Your Utopia

Praise for *Cursed Bunny*

"Bora Chung's *Cursed Bunny* mines those places where what we fear is true and what is true meet and separate and re-meet. The resulting stories are indelible. Haunting, funny, gross, terrifying—and yet when we reach the end, we just want more."

—Alexander Chee, author of *How to Write an Autobiographical Novel*

"Disturbing, chilling, wrenching, and absolute genius. I wanted Chung to write a story about a reader getting a deep look inside her fantastic swirling mind. I had to take breaks and gulps of air before plunging back into each story. Magnetic, eerie, immensely important."

—Frances Cha, author of *If I Had Your Face*

"Anton Hur's nimble translation manages to capture the tricky magic of Chung's voice—its wry humor and overarching coolness broken by sudden, thrilling dips into passages of vivid description. Even as Chung presents a catalog of grotesqueries that range from unsettling to seared-into-the-brain disturbing, her power is in restraint. She and Hur always keep the reader at a slight distance in order for the more chilling twists to land with maximum impact, allowing us to walk ourselves into the trap."

—*New York Times Book Review*

"[These] stories are beyond imagination: breathtaking, wild, crazy, the most original fiction I have ever encountered … each more astounding than the last."

—Louisa Ermelino, *Publishers Weekly*

"Like a family in a home, fantastic stories gather together in this book. The stories not only take their revenge, but also love you, and comfort you. You'll end up completely endeared to this fascinating collection!"

—Kyung-sook Shin, *New York Times* bestselling author of *Please Look After Mom* and *Violets*

"Sharp, wildly inventive, and slightly demented (in the most enjoyable way, of course) ... All we can say is buckle in, because when these stories take their horrific turn there's no setting them down."

—*Chicago Review of Books*

"[A] get-under-your-skin collection"

—*LitHub*

"Whether borrowing from fable, folktale, speculative fiction, science fiction, or horror, Chung's stories corkscrew toward devastating conclusions—bleak, yes, but also wise and honest about the nightmares of contemporary life. Don't read this book while eating—but don't skip these unflinching, intelligent stories, either."

—*Kirkus Reviews*, starred review

"Chung debuts with a well-crafted and horrifying collection of dark fairy tales, stark revenge fables, and disturbing body horror. Clever plot twists and sparkling prose abound. Chung's work is captivating and terrifying."

—*Publishers Weekly*

"The 10 stories, written between 1998 and 2016, span a variety of genres, flowing seamlessly from futuristic cautionary tales to surrealist, fable-like allegories inspired by Russian and Slavic tales."

—*The Boston Globe*

"Nothing concentrates the mind like Chung's terrors, which will shrivel you to a bouillon cube of your most primal instincts."

—*Vulture*

"This short story collection is like a car crash you can't look away from: grotesque in the best way ... Each story is fantastically unique, and unlike anything I've ever read before."

—*BuzzFeed*

"If you want a spooky set of stories that will crawl under your skin and burrow into your marrow and stay there forever, Chung's collection is a freaky, unforgettable outing. There's a folkloric quality to this collection, like these are urban legends that have finally been put to paper."

—*WIRED*

"The strange and everyday are melded in these startling and original tales ... *Cursed Bunny* is [Chung's] first book to be translated into English, and hopefully not the last."

—*San Francisco Chronicle*

Your Utopia

BORA CHUNG

Translated by Anton Hur

hachette
INDIA

This translation first published in 2024 by Honford Star Ltd

First published in India in 2024 by Hachette India
(Registered name: Hachette Book Publishing India Pvt. Ltd)
An Hachette UK company
www.hachetteindia.com

1

Print edition ISBN 978-93-5731-539-5
Ebook edition ISBN 978-93-5731-437-4

For sale in the Indian Subcontinent only.

Hachette Book Publishing India Pvt. Ltd
4th & 5th Floors, Corporate Centre,
Plot No. 94, Sector 44, Gurugram 122003, India

Printed and bound in India
by Manipal Technologies Limited

FSC www.fsc.org
MIX
Paper from responsible sources
FSC™ C043100

Contents

The Center for Immortality Research

"You know, I think I'm being stalked?"

That's what an unni at the Center confided to me two months ago, right in the middle of preparations for our anniversary event. Apparently, some man had called up the Center saying he was such-and-such and had come from the same region as my work unni and they were extremely close friends and he was running for the National Assembly and he would like to know the unni's phone number. Of course, our receptionist had immediately picked up on the fact that calling oneself "extremely close friends" with someone was extremely suspicious in itself, but when the mention of his political ambitions was followed by a presentation of his clearly fraudulent campaign promises, she cut him off, saying the unni was not at her desk right now and, furthermore, she was hardly in a position to hand out personal information such as phone numbers to strangers. Still, as a common courtesy, she had asked if he had any messages. This led to his "I'll call again later" follow-up calls, which made all other work almost impossible for the receptionist. Well, not that the Center had all that much work to be made impossible, normally, and this was the reception desk at that, but it *was* a very busy time. Everyone was frantic with the anniversary event, and how annoying that these calls, that could've been made during any of the vast expanses of emptiness in our calendars, were instead being foisted on us during *this* inopportune epoch.

If you were to ask what the Center for Immortality Research does, we do exactly what it says on the label: research immortality. In 1912, not long after Korea was forcibly annexed by Japan, the Center opened with the hopelessly silly slogan of "Our Country May Fall but We Shall Live Forever," and it was now the ninety-eighth year of its founding, which occasioned a huge blowout party. I still have no idea why we settled on ninety-eight for such an occasion instead of ninety or ninety-five or one hundred, but none of my older sunbaes at the Center know either, nor do the Center's board members no doubt. I mean, whatever, I'm at the bottom of the hierarchy in this establishment, and it's my job to do the work they give me, and if the work involves an anniversary party in a random year, that's what I've got to do.

I may be at the bottom of the hierarchy, but my title happens to be gwajang—"middle manager"—which of course is also part of a long chain of fluffed-up titles going right to the top. The board members are at the highest echelons, with a slew of bujangs and chajangs and other titles going down, and I'm the lowest-ranking, with not a single sawon below me, to say nothing of a daeli. Why, despite our designation as a research lab, we have such corporate titles instead of "primary investigator" or some such is also beyond me.

I mean, that's all well and good, especially when I get my monthly salary, but the problem is that because there are no sawons, all the tiny little chores that a sawon would do simply fall to me. And among the silly little chores I was given was to somehow get Movie Star B to come to our anniversary event.

Who was Movie Star B? He was in fact quite handsome and a good actor and had won some award and his name was well known; what did he have to do with our Center and its ninety-eighth anniversary? Well, nothing, except for the fact that a long time ago, before he became a big star, he had been in a fantasy movie that had to do with immortality. A movie that bombed so spectacularly that people these days hardly remembered its title, and the actors in it probably wanted to erase it from their CVs, but in any case, it was a movie about immortality, and the event would be filled with doctors and professors and fancy academics, which is why they thought having a movie star in the mix would make the atmosphere less rigid and the Center would look more glamorous, as it were, hence we decided to bring in Mr. B.

A good idea, but as all such planning goes, there was no way it was going to pass a board vote, and since all the bujangs and chajangs of the lab were experts in immortality in their own ways, there had to be a battle of what constitutes *immortality* as a concept before we moved forward. The Korean word for *immortality* is a combination of "long youth" and "forever life," and did "long" and "forever" really mean the same thing? Of course not, because "forever" lasted a lot longer than "long." Therefore, "long youth" was tawdry compared to "forever life," and for the actor to have starred in a movie about "long youth" was, according to detractors, not a good fit to the Center's mission. But when we then looked for movies dealing with the strictest sense of "forever life," there were almost no such films in Korea, and it would be absurd to think an actor like Hugh Jackman would bother to come to a Center for Immortality Research's ninety-eighth anniversary celebration event in Korea (there was also some debate as to whether the movie Hugh Jackman had starred in, *The Fountain,* was a movie about immortality or reincarnation, or whether it might actually have been about parallel universes, but when we decided to watch the film as a group in order to determine this issue, the board members all began to snore fifteen minutes into the film, making the whole point moot). Then, as an alternative, there was a Russian film trilogy that was extremely successful at the box office and won some impossible-to-pronounce award, but there was no one at the Center who could speak Russian and therefore this suggestion was also rejected.

And so, it came down to the actor Mr. B. When not a chajang or a bujang, or not even a board member, but the sojang himself suddenly called me, I ran to his office with my heart pounding; he handed me a Post-it with an email address and phone number scribbled on it and said such a famous movie star would probably have a busy schedule so I needed to call him early and nail him down, and that his assistant had already called them once and got a "We will look into the matter," and that this was the actor's manager's phone number and I needed to call them and get a sure answer, and he then proceeded to give me an exact script of what I was to say over the phone. I was to say I was the gwajang of a "large pharmaceutical company" and how we would appreciate it if you would grace our ninety-eighth anniversary celebrations with your presence, to be polite but firm, and to emphasize how we were a "major pharmaceutical company" and that I was a "gwajang." And that they'd understand they were being treated with a certain respect if they understood a gwajang was calling them, and also if I mentioned we were a big pharmaceutical company, they might think we would eventually offer him a commercial, which would make them hesitate to refuse the offer.

Of course, we were not a pharmaceutical company, but a research center attached to one, and we didn't do commercials, but in any case, this was the task I was given and I did it to the best of my abilities and it resulted in a complete and utter stonewalling from B's manager.

I made thirty-eight calls and sent twenty-two text messages and even fifteen really polite emails, but there was no answer, which made me anxious at first and then angry and, finally, resigned to the fact. Even if I was the lowest-ranking person and there was no possibility of moving up in this organization until the end of time, I had managed to hold on to this job all these years and it just riled me that I was suddenly faced with an obstacle that had nothing to do with my office work or research, but something as silly as a manager refusing to take my calls, it was all just incredibly unfair.

As I sat in the Center lobby, fiddling with my phone and wondering if I should try again, suddenly I heard a voice.

"Excuse me, you don't happen to know where Kim Segyeong bujang's office is?"

The man was very polite and his tone very calm, and when I looked up and met his gaze I had a feeling I had seen his face somewhere before, but I couldn't quite put my finger on it.

"Do you know what floor Kim Segyeong's office is? I am a

childhood friend of hers, Park Hyukseh, I'm running for the National Assembly ..."

That's when I thought, *Oh, it's the stalker,* words that almost left my mouth, but I stopped myself. Whereupon I frantically rummaged through my mind to find something else to say but came up completely empty. And since I simply stared at him, the man spoke again.

"I was very close with Kim Segyeong bujang since we were children and grew up in the same place, and I do have some connection with the Center. As a candidate for the National Assembly, I am working day and night for the betterment of my country and fellow countrymen. If you pick me as your National Assembly member, I will make everyone in our country live forever, and that would make the Center for Immortality Research the foremost research center in the land ..."

Make everyone in the country immortal? I've heard all sorts of things from politicians in my time, but this took the cake. However, my academic curiosity forced me to keep listening to his spiel no matter how ridiculous it got.

At the end of it I blurted, "But how exactly are you going to achieve immortality for all?"

I'm sure I was the only person in this entire century who had showed that much interest, little as it was, in his campaign promises. He got all excited and began to speak in a louder voice, his eyes positively sparkling.

"The twenty-first century is the age of technology, is it not? Concentrating all our technology to compress the sun's rays and shoot them onto Earth to make our ancestors come alive again would be my first task. The method was already developed in mid-nineteenth-century Russia and was thoughtified to be impossible to bring to fruition at the time …"

Thoughtified? Was he making up grammar now? I loathe people who go to great lengths to keep talking in the passive voice, but there was no way of stopping the deluge that was coming at me now.

"Of course, our ancestors who have been deceased for relatively longer periods of time and are skeletons now might be thoughtified to be difficult to revive, but the ones who have just died and whose bodies are in passable condition will not be too difficult to bring back, I should think. To restore our dead ancestors and put them on the path to immortality in its own way can be thoughtified as a form of ancestral piety and befitting our country's traditions that speak of respecting our elders, and it is also a way of maintaining and even increasing our population which is decreasing rapidly due to declining birth rates—"

"Excuse me." The campaign promise was one thing, but if I kept hearing this "thoughtified" word one more time, I thoughtified I would never manage to hold on to my sanity. "I have to go back to my office. I'll tell Kim Segyeong bujang you're here."

But unfortunately for me and my attempts to escape, the world *office* made his whole face light up.

"You're going to your office? I shall go with you. So Kim Segyeong must be in the office today, is she?"

"No. That unni—I mean, Kim Segyeong bujang is working outside the office today and she's not here."

As abruptly as it had lit up, a shadow fell over the man's face.

"Oh, she's not here again? She must be really busy. Where *is* she working so busily these days?"

"She really is ..." Out of desperation, I began to lie extemporaneously. "We're actually ... going to have an anniversary event for the founding of our Center, and we were going to invite Movie Star B to the ceremony, but we can't get a hold of him. ... So I think she's at the manager's office, trying to negotiate, but I don't think it's going well—"

"Is that so?"

It had been a lie, but his face became so sincere that I began to worry. Lo and behold, the man started interrogating me about the issue.

"Why isn't the negotiation thoughtified to be going well? Is it a money issue? Schedule clashes?"

"Well, I actually don't know myself ..." It's true that people say the wildest things the more anxious they get, but in this case, I want to blame the weird reappearance of *thoughtified* for throwing me off. "So like ... when Unni first went to their office, she didn't call him 'Seonsengnim' but simply called him 'Mister' and ... so ..."

"What? He refused the invitation on such a trivial an issue?"

He looked so angry that I wanted to take back what I'd just said, but it was too late. As I hesitated, trying to figure out what to say next, the man's face hardened and said, "All right. I'll do something about it. So you're saying Kim Segyeong bujang is at that actor's management office, am I correct?"

"Well ... yes ..."

Of course, Unni was calmly sitting in her office on the fourth floor at that moment, suffering from anniversary event-related activities that had nothing to do with immortality, and neither of us had any idea where such-and-such actor's management office was. But the man seemed satisfied and left after saying goodbye, which was a great relief, and I forgot about the whole thing soon after.

Until a month later when I was reminded of it because of the election. So that guy, who claimed to be running for the National Assembly and had that ridiculous platform, the guy who had pursued Unni so zealously without it ever being clear as to why, turned out to be an actual National Assembly candidate, and what's even more incomprehensible, he actually became electedified.

And then that actor B's manager actually called our office. They were, surprisingly, agreeing to attend the anniversary event and were asking for the place and time. I was pretty sure the man on the other end of the line was the manager whom I'd called thirty-eight times with no answer, and him being "delighted" to have B attend did not exactly sound sincere. I felt a sudden sense of desperation and very apologetically told him the time and place and how to get here, but the manager cut me off at one point as if impatient to get off the phone. But even after being so abruptly cut off, I couldn't help but stare at the receiver in a daze. Unni's stalker, who had actually won his election, had believed my lies (which weren't 100 percent lies, to be fair) and as soon as he won his election had, out of affection for her, used his stalker powers on actor B, on B's manager, and even on B's manager's boss, throwing his political power in their faces a little, using all sorts of threats and insinuations to somehow get B to swear on his life he would attend the event. I was a little miffed that I hadn't known all this before and had acted so obsequiously to the manager during our phone call, since he did ignore me thirty-eight times and this had been a chance to ride a National Assembly member's coattails to an emotionally satisfying conclusion.

These little and big incidents made our event planning creak along. Now that I had successfully gotten B to participate, the next thing I had to do was make invitations and posters. I accepted this chore, since I was in no position as the lowest of the low to deny the highest of the high, but later I learned all too well that these invitations and posters were to be distributed outside of our organization and furthermore would leave important material evidence in the form of real letters printed on real paper, which meant if I did well no one cared and if I made a mistake the whole world would know. I wouldn't have the tiniest bit of authority, only loads and loads of responsibility, and my public humiliation was more or less inevitable, which is how it turned out in the end.

It went something like this. I was asked to write the invite copy titled "A Letter of Invitation," and so I tried my best to put together the most polite and succinct invite that I could. The board members took a look at it and it went up to the sojang at the top. The office of the sojang passed on his comments.

"Don't say 'letter,' say 'words.'"

So I changed it to "Words of Invitation." Board member A gave me the following order:

"Change 'of Invitation' to 'Inviting.'"

So I changed it to "Inviting Words." Then board member B ordered:

"Change 'words' to 'letter.'"

That, I could not change.

"Uh, sir, it was the sojang who changed that word …"

"Oh, really? Then leave it the way it is."

Exactly three minutes and twenty seconds later, C gave me a call.

"Change 'inviting' to 'invitation.'"

By the way, the invitation in question was half a page long. I was getting to the point of wanting to put the latest draft in my mouth before jumping off a bridge. But what could I do? I was a team player and what's more, a salary-receiver, which meant I had to see this through no matter what. The person who really suffered after the invitation was finalized and the poster had to be designed and approved was the graphic designer.

This graphic designer was the high school friend of a cousin of the husband of an unni of a person I knew at one of the headquarters' subcontractors, in other words someone I could say was a personal acquaintance but not really at the same time. The reason I didn't even bother looking at her portfolio before hiring her was that we were in a rush. I wanted to at least print out the invitations to give them to the VIPs to RSVP. But asking the person I knew at one of the headquarters' subcontractors to call their unni to ask their husband to call their cousin to ask their friend the graphic designer took a bit of time to arrange, not to mention the time it took for the designer to call back their friend who would call their cousin to tell the unni's husband to tell the unni to call the subcontractor to call me, which led me to finally calling the designer on a Friday to tell her I needed to hand over the files to the printer on Monday no matter what, which meant she needed to work through the weekend, and the whole while I assumed she would say this was impossible.

But the designer actually came up with a finished design. Not only that, but I'd given her the job on a Friday and she called me on Saturday to say she was done. I thought it looked perfect and there would be no problem simply handing it to the printer. I sent it out to the sojang and the board members. That was Saturday night.

There was no response until Sunday evening, when the calls began.

Board Member F: Move the Center logo a little to the left.

I moved it.

Board Member G: Move the Center logo a little further up.

I moved it.

Board Member D: Left-align "Inviting Words."

I left-aligned it.

Board Member A: Right-align "Inviting Words" and move the Center logo to the right.

I right-aligned and moved it.

Board Member C: I told you to change "Inviting Words" to "Letter of Invitation," why didn't you fix it?

I'd told this guy the sojang himself had changed "letter" to "words" ages ago, why was he getting on my case now? But I couldn't tell a board member that he was getting on anything even resembling my case, so I had to explain everything to him one more time.

Board member E: Get rid of the background picture.

I got rid of it.

Board member A: Why did you get rid of that background picture? Put it back.

And there were many other orders, but I think you get the idea.

The designer was kind enough to fix everything we asked her to fix, but at my sixth phone call, she very carefully asked me, "So, I think we'll continue to get requests like this up until we go to the printers tomorrow … Do you think it'll be easier for both of us if you just came to my studio instead of calling me each time?"

And so, I found myself going to the designer's studio in the middle of our Sunday night. It was cozy and her coffee smelled lovely and more than that she had two nimble and affectionate cats, which made it a nice work environment, but the poor designer was being bombarded with a call every three minutes, being asked to move the logo to the left or to the right, the words up and down the page, all night, until finally when the gray light of dawn slipped through the curtains, she said to me, "Is all the work you do at the Center run like this?" Seeing how pale her face and bloodshot her eyes were, I realized that while I was a mere lowest of the low working at near-volunteer wages at the Center, I was going to do my best to get the designer the highest pay we could offer her.

As I tortured our poor graphic designer in this fruitless quest, were the other bujangs and chajangs just twiddling their thumbs? No, they were going round and round in their own circles of hell. The Center was going to do some kind of exhibit with headquarters, something to do with immortality, and of course this idea did not come from headquarters but the Center, and headquarters' attitude was basically *we paid for the stupid thing already why are you bothering us with this*, complete disinterest in other words, which meant every time the Center had to contact them and get approval for getting a venue and display items and creating a real exhibit that was worthy of the pharma brand, it was a huge mountain of disapproval to climb every time. The fact that bujangs and chajangs of one of our country's major pharmaceutical brands' research centers were going through this ridiculous amount of work was completely ludicrous, but what can you do? Like I said before, we really had no sawon under us and the lowest of the low was stuck in a graphic designer's studio moving a logo around a poster, and even if we were a part of a big pharmaceutical company, we were still just a research center and not a profit-creating department like sales, meaning we've got to make do with what little event-planning budget headquarters tossed at us and not even dream of outsourcing the work.

Finally, we were two days away from the anniversary event and exhibit, created by the blood, sweat, and tears of all the people working at the Center and our poor graphic designer who through no fault of her own got mired in this mess. The invitations, posters, and ads for the top-five major dailies all finished, I found myself having nothing to do, so I went to the event space to help out, where I happened to meet Kim Segyeong bujang, the unni who was being stalked. We worked on the same fourth floor of the Center but were so busy with our respective event planning that we had had no time to talk to each other for a while now, but we were able to go to lunch together that day, where I voiced my biggest concern about her, that of the stalker, but surprisingly, she seemed completely unfazed about it.

"It's all right. It turns out, he's on our side."

"What? What do you mean?"

Unni smiled. "It's been such a long time, you must've forgotten?"

Forgotten what? Unni must've seen the question on my face, because she explained, "He used to work for the Center, very briefly, a while ago."

Really?

"I'm telling you. Maybe he quit around the time you came in. But I think your times overlapped for about two months. You really don't remember?"

Now that I thought about it, there was someone like him who had quit not soon after I joined. Was that why his face was so familiar?

"Then is it true he's from the same region as you? Why did he stalk you?"

"He really is from the same place as me. I think we used to go hiking together and see the tigers and such."

"Then what is up with his weird campaign promise?" I asked, still not convinced of his good intentions.

Unni laughed. "That's an actual theory that existed in late nineteenth-century Russia. I don't remember the guy's name, he was some kind of philosopher, and the idea was a sensation at the time. The philosopher still has fanatic adherents in Russia, I believe."

To compress the energy of the sun and revive our ancestors into immortal beings, and to not only believe such things but to be a fanatic adherent of it—Russia must be a very strange place. Unni, seeing my expression, laughed again.

"That man, he's always had a comedic streak, but he really believes in immortality. It's just that he didn't want to study it, he wanted to apply it in real life, and that's where we diverged in our attitudes. Still, he must've heard somewhere that we were doing a ninety-eighth anniversary event. I'm sure he's here to see some old friends and glad-hand and all that."

Then he should've said that from the beginning, why did he have to single out Kim Segyeong bujang and seem like a stalker? But Unni looked perfectly at peace with the whole thing.

"Also," she added, "he really was helpful, wasn't he? That whole actor thing, he took care of that. And the celebrity lecturer, too, he got her for us."

"A celebrity what?"

"She lectures about immortality from the perspectives of medicine, religion, and philosophy, a three-part talk."

Well, Unni seemed fine, and so I decided to be fine about it myself, and we were running out of lunch time so we quickly finished our food. And so two more days passed, and it was finally the day of the anniversary event.

The ceremony was at 6 p.m., but the event space was already crowded by morning. We were using the hall in the basement of headquarters, and usually it was a dark and dreary place, but with the lights shining brightly for the event and the people crowding about, it actually looked pretty festive. Especially when Movie Star B arrived—the mood turned to a near frenzy. B didn't look like he wanted to be there, but when Park Hyeokse, Unni's stalker and sitting National Assembly member, came and asked to shake B's hand, the sight of the actor's disgusted face as he complied made all the stress I felt while preparing the event somehow just fly away.

Furthermore, there was an extraordinarily beautiful woman with long black hair coming down to her waist who made quite an impression on everyone. I assumed she was an actor like B, but apparently she was the celebrity lecturer hired by Park Hyeokse. Which is apparently why Park went to her side and spoke to her and tried to make her feel more at home, but the lecturer herself seemed bored and disgruntled to be surrounded by so many strangers. She walked around the exhibit space a bit but did not seem interested in the exhibits.

The exhibition itself, however, was pretty neat. When they first announced it was being done, I wondered how on Earth could they fill up that wide of an exhibition space with things that supposedly had something to do with immortality, but there really was a whole plethora of things, like paintings, photographs, books, DVDs, and other interesting objects. Of course, some of the paintings were by unknown painters who had produced blobs with titles like "No Death" and whatnot, but there were other artworks that had to do with religious immortality or resurrection, and a documentary series on DVD about the Emperor Qin Shi Huang and his quest to find the herb of immortality (a personal possession of the board member who had insisted "long youth" and "forever life" were the same thing), and looking around the fancily decorated exhibition hall, I could see how obsessed humanity had been with living forever and how this obsession had continued from the dawn of history to today, which was awe-inspiring on one hand and, I don't know, pitiable on the other, a complicated combination of emotions.

The books, CDs, and DVDs were in display cases, and I was selling pretty bottles with our Center label stuck on them that purportedly contained "Immortality Elixir" as a souvenir—five thousand won a pop—because we couldn't afford to hire a temp for the job.

"This isn't really some kind of immortality elixir, right?" I asked the chajang who was sitting next to me at the souvenir table.

He grinned. "I think maybe two out of the fifteen hundred are the real thing?"

"You don't think people are buying this and thinking it's actually what it says on the label, do you?"

"No one believes in that kind of thing in these enlightened times. The people who buy them are subcontractors or from headquarters, throwing us some pocket change to be nice and help us save face."

Considering how they were just being "nice," sales of these bottles throughout the whole day amounted to 300,000 won, perhaps thanks to how cute the bottle looked with its label (for which we had made our poor graphic designer stay up three nights straight, asking her to move it now to the left, now to the right).

"Well, I'm glad they're selling."

"They better be selling. We have to sell all these so we can turn a profit and pay off that graphic designer of yours."

I was surprised. "We still haven't paid her?"

In lieu of an answer, the chajang pointed outside. At the entrance there were people from the catering company bussing in food, setting up a banquet.

"We've long used up our budget from headquarters. We'll keep selling all the bottles we've made and pay off the graphic designer in installments."

He picked up the money and counted the various thousand and five thousand won bills. "There's two hundred and ninety-eight thousand won in here. Transfer this to her now, and we'll give her some more tomorrow when we sell more."

I thought he was joking, but he wasn't. I'd never been more mortified in my life. Also, he never explained why, despite the bottles being five thousand won each, he had ended up with a value that ended with eight thousand won, but I was too scared at that point to ask.

Soon it became evening, and the anniversary event began. The ceremony itself was, as expected, completely boring. Some people from headquarters and former sojangs went up to give speeches that began with, "My dear Center family ..." and really seemed to require immortality itself to get through completely. The VIPs who could doze off without consequence dozed off without consequence.

With the formalities over with, the current sojang finally declared, "Shall we move on to the lobby and enjoy the banquet?" and all the dozing VIPs immediately leaped to their feet and made a beeline for the banquet hall. After all the bujangs and chajangs left, it was my turn to switch off the lights of the exhibition space and close the door behind me. I couldn't lock it behind me because everyone had left their things in the event space, and I didn't want to be getting up every ten seconds in the middle of my own dinner to open the door for someone who wanted the Chapstick in their purse.

So I was furtively eating from my own plate at the banquet, a really nice meal considering we spent all the headquarters' money on the catering, and the wine wasn't too bad, either. Of course, I was the lowest of the low and didn't have the freedom to drink at an event whether there was drink available or not, but I did manage to pour myself one glass and sip away in a corner.

"Are you Chung gwajang, the one who was in charge of the invitations?"

The voice came from *right behind me* and I almost spewed my wine.

"What? Uh, yes—"

"They came out rather nicely. Good job."

I felt a rush of pride. "Well, it was really the designer who—"

"Anyway," butted in Board Member A as he looked around and lowered his voice, "you seem to have written 'Inviting Wonds' instead of 'Inviting Words.'"

"What?"

The board member took out a crumpled invitation from his pocket, spread it open, and pointed at the title with his index finger. As my face contorted with horror, he added, "It's all right, you can hardly see it. The invitation is very pretty, so ... good job."

Then, board member A swanned off to schmooze with the other VIPs.

The other five board members proceeded to corner me one by one to inform me of the same thing in the same order, with slight variations: "Are you Chung gwajang, the one in charge of the invitations? They came out rather nicely. But"—looking around and lowering their voices—"you've spelled *established* as 'establiched.'" "*Grace us* as 'graze us.'" "*Thank you* as 'Thark you.'" "It's all right, you can hardly see it. The invitation is very pretty ..."

And so, after this barrage of consoling or berating, I was completely demoralized by the time Board Member D sidled up to me crouched in the corner, and I followed him when he asked me to follow him, thinking I was finally getting fired, steeling myself for the inevitable. But against my expectations, D went right up to the door of the event hall and said, "Got a key? Open this."

"It's, uh, not locked—"

"Oh? Follow me then."

D opened the door and strode inside. As I was about to turn the light on, D told me not to bother and crossed the hall to where the display cases were.

"Chung gwajang, be on the lookout."

"Be on the what, now?"

Was he … going to shoot someone in the hall? No, he was opening the display case and stuffing the DVDs about Qin Shi Huang in a bag.

"That asshole F, going on about 'long youth' and 'forever life' like they're the same thing … Selling out to television shows just to show off, what kind of a fucking researcher does he think that is … Not even giving me a complimentary DVD set when it came out …"

As D mumbled on, I kept hearing a rustling sound behind me, and I was filled with fear. D grabbed each of the five DVDs and put them in his bag, after which he strode out of the dark room with me following him. And when we returned to the banquet, the whole place was in chaos because an attacker had descended upon it.

The attacker kept screaming something incomprehensible

as he held up an electric iron in one hand and something that looked like Febreze in the other, running around the banquet setup pushing people, and the event being on a Friday night the security guards had already gone home or out to dinner. It took some time, therefore, to subdue him. The expensive food was scattered all over the place (I hadn't eaten properly all day because of the preparations and so this fact was the first to register with me), and the attacker kept saying something that sounded like "I WANT TO DO IT" and what might have been a person's name as he jumped around, and listening carefully I thought the name could be the lecturer's name, the one invited by Park Hyeokse, which made everyone turn to look for her but she had disappeared.

Meanwhile, some brave folks from headquarters and the Center took it upon themselves to restrain the man, but the attacker was so all over the place that it wasn't as easy as it sounds. Someone had called the police, but they took their sweet time getting here, and it was a clever worker at headquarters who brought down a tranquilizer from upstairs (this being a pharmaceutical company), though the sight of the tranquilizer bottle and syringe made the attacker even more frenzied, spraying the Febreze all over the place and making evasive maneuvers, catching one of the workers from headquarters in a headlock, who looked like he would get his neck broken—but in a demonstration of incredible flexibility, the worker managed to reach around and jab the attacker's butt with the tranquilizer. By the time the police arrived, the man was snoring, and the four police officers took hold of a limb each and carried him out of the lobby (syringe still stuck in his butt), but the attendees were too rattled to go on with the event and went home, ending the day faster than expected, to my immense satisfaction, but then I got a call from the police the next morning, which was a Saturday, and this foreshadowed my spending the entire weekend in and out of the police station.

The attacker claimed to be the boyfriend of the celebrity lecturer, and he had suspected she was having an affair with a "tall and handsome man" and pretending to be giving lectures so she could meet this other guy and he had seen her go into a building with a "tall and handsome man" and that had made him lose his sanity, hence the mayhem that followed. The lecturer claimed she had no idea who this man was at first, but he presented proof they knew each other, so she then claimed he was her "ex-boyfriend" but the iron and Febreze were actually her possessions and she would like them back, please, but apparently they were evidence and she was denied their return.

And so the weekend passed and it was Monday, and we had to clean up the exhibition of the ninety-eighth anniversary of our Center, and while we were packing up, it was discovered that Board Member F's DVD series was gone.

Chaos akin to when the attacker had broken in ensued. Everything we had just packed was unpacked, which took a whole extra day. When no DVD series was discovered despite these efforts, someone suggested we look at the CCTV footage. Having had no idea there was CCTV in this place, I turned pale as a sheet and tried to steer them away from the idea, but while the DVD series was complimentary it was worth twenty thousand won per disc, technically, and 100,000 won in all, and Board Member F was stomping his feet saying he must have justice as the DVDs were out of print and completely irreplaceable, which was how he managed to overcome the reluctance of the building security team to review the footage. Needless to say, my face was all over it.

While D was stealing F's DVDs, and I was on the lookout, the little red light behind me had been a CCTV camera. There I was, looking straight into the red light of the camera without knowing what it was, practically engraving my face into the evidence. The camera caught me from a higher angle, I was looking up, and the light was just right so there wasn't a flaw on my face, and I was dismayed that I'd look so good in *this* footage of all places but a little part of me thought, I *did* look good, which made me giggle. And as F and all the bujangs and chajangs glared at me, I couldn't stop myself from giggling. Meanwhile, D, the one who had *actually* stolen the DVDs, was moving with his face behind my shoulder, which made him invisible to the camera. It was unlucky of me, or lucky of me depending on how you looked at it, and I realized that no good would come of pitting the board members against each other, which was why despite threats and entreaties I refused to divulge the identity of the board member hidden behind me.

And also … over my shoulder, next to D stealing the DVDs, there was something gray there: a person's face, whom everyone now surmised was an accessory to the crime, so F demanded the security team at headquarters zoom in on that spot (I thought that was something they only did in American crime procedurals), and in that photo we could see Movie Star B and the beautiful celebrity lecturer holding hands and looking very frightened.

And so ended the Center for Immortality Research's ninety-eighth anniversary event. The culprit of the DVD theft was never discovered, and I just wasted a lot of my time being called here and there about the whole mess. The DVDs in question had been printed as a limited edition by the broadcasting company that produced them, and F was correct in that they were basically irreplaceable. From then on, F's face would turn into a grimace whenever he bumped into me, but there was nothing I could do about that.

National Assembly member Park Hyeokse also fell out of contact after that. My guess is that he had wanted to get into a little something with the beautiful celebrity lecturer, but he had only ended up bringing her into the clutches of Movie Star B, which must've hurt his pride. I have no idea what happened to the lecturer, but Movie Star B seems to have stopped working.

I later read some article about an attacker showing up at B's door, kicking it, holding an electric iron and what seemed to be a USB cable, screaming, "All tall and handsome men must die!" until the police came and he made a run for it. The man was not caught, but aside from the dented door there were no real damages, and B did not seem particularly eager for the police to find him, and so the whole case was dropped.

And I continue to stumble through work at the Center for Immortality Research.

To be the lowest of the low and an accessory to the burglary of a board member's precious possession—this bravery or stupidity was not enough to get me fired, because research centers being the kind of places that they are, it's almost impossible to fire anyone, and aside from that I know a secret. Everyone at the Center knows the secret. The secret is that we really are immortal.

I was born in 1914, and in the year I turned twenty I joined "Long Life Pharmacy" as a trainee, where I accidentally was given an immortality elixir, whereupon I became young forever and ended up at this research center. I'm not going anywhere. There's nowhere else for me to go, and more than anything else, I don't have the confidence to create a new life away from these other people who are also forever young and forever alive. From the sojang at the very top and downward, none of the employees at the Center can ever leave, for the same reasons.

And so, just as they said in the speeches at the anniversary event, we really are a family. You can quit a company or disown a friend, but you can't quit or disown your family. Like they said in the founding of the Center, we can lose our country but we were still going to live forever, and the world may end but we were always going to be entangled in each other's lives.

There are people who find solace in ties that we can never sever. If those ties have to do with making a living, the sense of stability must double. But sitting in the lobby of the Center and watching the people come and go, right before going up to work myself, I suddenly had a scary and sad thought. As long as I lived, I had to figure out a way to put food on the table, and this eternal need to feed myself was frightening, and how this need would persist to our 198th, 298th, 398th anniversaries ... and how I would have no choice but to spend all that time in this Center, made me sadder and more scared than anything else in the world. But if you thought about it, whether you were forever young or not, anyone who had to make their own living was in the same boat as I was.

Not that the thought makes me feel any better.

The End of the Voyage

I lost my friend.

I was standing on the rubble of a fallen world, looking around me. The only warm thing was the sunlight. The concrete debris I was sitting on was hot to the touch because of it. But that was all.

As far as the eye could see, there was only shattered concrete, twisted steel bars, broken bricks, and cracked asphalt. There wasn't so much as a tree or a blade of grass, much less a living animal. The sky was clear and the clouds looked peaceful, but the sun poured down its light on a landscape that was nothing less than desolate.

Should I go back to the spaceship?

I looked up at the sky. It was blinding.

The sunlight was pure but the air was cold. Who knew how long the sun would be up there, and what would come out in the night of this changed world. Every breeze was like a stab of cold into the folds of my clothing. Goosebumps dotted the nape of my neck.

Still, the sun was out, and the concrete I was sitting on remained warm. I decided to sit for a little while longer, enjoying the heat.

But I had to go back to the spaceship eventually. I knew that. Just a few more minutes and I was bound to get thirsty. And then after a while, hungry. The day would darken soon. There was nothing to eat here, nothing to drink. No way of obtaining food or drink, either. There wasn't anything that was alive. The ship at least had water and electricity.

And him.

I sighed a little.

The Disease started spreading about four years and eight months ago, by my estimate. There's no way of knowing how long it's been in Earth time.

Nor is there a way of determining who was the first person infected or how. There was that small-town family in Iowa, a mother and father and three children, where only the oldest son survived. They're the official first infected people of the Disease. The eldest son in question went to school as always, and during lunchtime, very matter-of-factly, tried to take a bite out of the arm of the student sitting next to him; this was when the Disease became public knowledge. The eldest son claimed that the other student had "offered" his arm by "placing it so obviously" for him that he thought he was "being invited to take a bite." "That's why my mom ate my sister's arm, and it was fine to do," which is why the principal called 911. They found the bodies of the eldest son's parents, younger sister, and younger brother—well, parts of each. The autopsy coupled with the eldest son's testimony concluded that the father probably had the Disease first, then the wife, then the couple ate the daughter, then each other, and the eldest eventually contracted it and ate his brother.

There wasn't much left, however, to do an autopsy on, which was why they could not determine the exact times of death.

Whether it was a matter of could not or would not was uncertain, but military intelligence and the Iowa police said only that much and no more. The eldest son in question was quarantined in a facility. A tabloid reported that he spoke about his family and had a sad expression and cried, but when asked if he had eaten his family as well, he answered, "Of course," like it was nothing. When asked how could he have done such a thing if he loved his family, he said, "Eating just an arm or a leg won't kill them, right?" as if discussing the weather. Then why hadn't he thought his brother would die when he ate his heart? "Well, that wasn't his heart," he said cryptically. What did he mean by that? "You know ... [insert many more evasive filler phrases of a similar nature here]." No, I didn't know what he meant by that. From then on, silence.

Because this was a tabloid publication famous for fabricating stories, it was hard to take it too seriously. But if any part of it were true, then I would say it shows very well how people infected with the Disease behave. Aside from the afflicted's tendency to regard other people as food, they were completely normal. Or at least, behaved and conversed like they were. It was only when cannibalism was mentioned in conversation that they responded abnormally, most notably their uniform insistence that eating people did not kill the eaten. Whether they knew but were in denial because of their uncontrollable appetites or whether it was a neurological symptom of the Disease was something scholars of medicine all over the world would argue about later on, but they never came to a conclusion. Mostly because the

Disease spread quicker than they could arrive at any consensus.

The Disease seemed to spread through every possible method. When bitten by an afflicted person, the likelihood of infection (assuming they weren't killed) was 100 percent. Sharing food with the afflicted had a 70 to 80 percent chance of infection. Being in the same room had lower chances of infection, but it was still around 50 percent. There were no reports of sneezing or coughing when it came to symptoms, which meant bodily fluids seemed less of a risk, but there was no way to be sure.

The really disconcerting thing was that it was impossible to tell who was infected until the moment they tried to eat someone. The afflicted did not seem to recognize each other either. It's not like they charged at you screaming in hunger; like the eldest son in the first public case, they tended to casually take a bite out of someone who happened to be right next to them. There were instances where they would refrain from doing so, like if they happened to be full or thought they would be in danger. The afflicted tended to be in denial about their affliction and denied the existence of the Disease altogether. And because there were no signs upon infection and no visible symptoms in the beginning, there was no way of determining the latency period that the virus lay in wait. There was also the high chance of infection among the doctors who treated the afflicted—medical researchers, police investigating the cannibalism cases, and journalists reporting on the incidents on the ground being infected as well. It was impossible to trust anyone. The only thing you could trust was that the Disease existed and anyone physically close by could be taking a bite out of you at any moment.

And that's how a disease that started in a little town in Iowa very quickly, but also silently, spread throughout the country. The students, teachers, and administrators at the eldest son's school, the work colleagues of the parents, and the 911 medics and police who responded to their call were the first to be infected. Not only were those who fled the town to avoid the Disease themselves infected but they proved instrumental in spreading the Disease elsewhere. Because of the peculiarities of the American federal system, where each state is almost run like an independent country, it took ages for the incidents in Iowa to be connected to those of the six states that bordered it, and even longer for the federal government to finally do something about it. Nearby Illinois's city of Chicago was especially consequential because once the Disease took over there, airplanes carried it across America and to the rest of the world.

And so it came to pass that all of civilization began trying to eat each other. Perhaps it would've been better if, like in a zombie movie, reanimated corpses were walking around in flocks, screaming as they went for the kill. Instead, perfectly normal-looking people went about politely conversing and smiling and would suddenly crush the skull of someone nearby and chop them up into edible sections and, packing them in brown paper bags to eat on a park bench, would then watch the sunlight on the grass, peacefully nibbling a human liver. There were many measures put in place, from the family level to the national, but because the people involved in implementing such measures were often either infected or would be soon enough, they fell woefully short.

Of those measures, one that required international cooperation was a mission to send up into space a group of uninfected.

There was no real discussion as to what would happen to them once they were in space; find an alien civilization and get help? The chances were so miniscule, you might as well be filming a science fiction movie. No, it was much better to make a run for it. The plan was simply that as many uninfected people as possible should escape for now and lay low for a while and return when the situation died down on Earth or some other solution was discovered.

This project, somewhat inappropriately named Project Noah's Ark, was of course undertaken under extreme secrecy. Still, the powerful people who managed to get wind of the project tried to get themselves on it, but the right to board was only given to those who had passed numerous tests to ensure they were not infected, and of these, aside from the very few people who were able to pilot spaceships and navigate space, only those with expertise in medicine, biology, chemistry, or pharmacology were accepted.

While I did work for the Department of Defense, I was really a linguistics specialist who was hired to break codes; I have no idea how I ended up on the spaceship. My official remit was, in case we ran into aliens while we were up there, to find a way to communicate with extraterrestrials, but this was, no matter how you looked at it, some nonsense proposed by an official who had read too much science fiction. While I did regularly scan various incoming signals from space in case we were being hailed, my primary job was to keep in contact with my government. Various control towers on Earth transmitted the progress of the Disease in their countries to the spaceship, such as increases or decreases in the numbers of afflicted or what their country's latest measures were. I collected this information, along with the research results produced in our spaceship being passed on by the captain—who was from the same country as me—and sent it along in code to my country. It was said the whole world was working together to rid the world of the Disease, but surely it was better for *my* country to find a cure before anyone else. The spaceship had also been built and launched from my country, so of course it was understandable that my country would want first dibs on any pertinent information. But I emphasize that this extra bit of subterfuge was conducted under the strictest secrecy, and I was to share none of it with anyone on board except the captain.

Watching the sun going down, as I hugged my knees on the concrete that still retained some of the heat of the day despite the descending chill, I wondered not about the possibilities of communication but the impossibilities of meaning being conveyed from one individual to another.

There is no such thing as two-way communication. That's what I learned after spending most of my waking hours coding and decoding communiqués. The purest form of communication is one-sided infodumps. Things like commands or reports. These communications are done in the simplest way possible to avoid misunderstandings.

I loved that simplicity. Seeing computers use my algorithms to decipher a code that looked completely meaningless as valuable information that only my side could comprehend made me feel in my bones the full meaning of the word "communication." There was also a kind of wicked, lip-curling satisfaction in transforming information that would be valuable to the other side into something they couldn't understand. There I was in the point where the possibility and impossibility of communication met, carefully scoping out the potentials of either side. But I never, in the end, trusted the process wholeheartedly.

Most of the people on the spaceship were doctors or scientists or spaceflight engineers. I was, in other words, a very exceptional case among them. Every time I attempted to converse with them, I would retreat after concluding the STEM mind not only thought differently but was probably structured differently to begin with. And the fact that I also had a secret mission on top of my official status made me even more isolated on the ship. The other passengers, like the engineers, worked in shifts for the most part. Everyone on the ship knew who was on their shift as they would report every changing of the guard, exchanging greetings. The doctors and scientists also had the common objective of curing the Disease and often shared their findings with each other, and those who found they worked well together would create new teams. The only thing I was allowed to say even under the most persistent of questioning was that I was "in charge of communication," and I was only seen silently going in and out of the captain's ready room, so it looked like I was only kissing up to the captain and was antisocial and furthermore uncooperative and not to be trusted. I eventually became someone to avoid on the ship, but human beings can adapt to almost any change, and in a lot of ways this made my job much easier anyway. Still, I did have feelings, and I couldn't say that everyone keeping me at a distance didn't make me feel bad at all.

The only passenger or crew who didn't ostracize me was this guy.

This guy was a space mechanic. Like most mechanics, he was not part of the military but an air force subcontractor in his country. (Well, most of the crew and passengers on this ship were civilians, really. The captain had been part of our department of defense like I'd been, but the fact that there were no other military or ex-military personnel under the rank of first mate would always strangely bother me.) But apparently, even civilians divided themselves into ranks according to seniority and skill, and this guy looked like he was near the bottom of the hierarchy. Also, in contrast to the image one normally thought of when hearing the words "space mechanic," he was a rather sensitive and fragile soul, easily hurt by the dry and businesslike dealings of the other mechanics. He was, in other words, somewhat ostracized himself. That's how we befriended each other.

Aside from the fact that he was constantly being pushed out of the herd he was a part of, we really didn't have much in common. I was a linguist, he was a mechanic. My interests lay in trying to express, compress, and convert the information I knew in the most simple and effective manner in order to transmit it. His interest was mostly which component of the spaceship was malfunctioning and how to go about fixing it. He had a tendency to try to always explain what he was doing. About halfway into the second sentence of his explanations, I gave up trying to understand. Similarly, I tried to explain to him the basic structures of language (I mean, I couldn't tell him what I was really doing there), but the best he could do was to regard things like "subject" and "verb" and "object" as components of a machine to assemble to create this thing called language. I did try to explain to him that creating a sentence wasn't as simple as that and the parts of speech behaved differently according to the language being spoken, but his expression told me it was meaningless to try to explain, so I gave up at some point. Still, he found my silly little explanations very fascinating and listened to all of them without any criticism or disagreement. Because he seemed to be interested in whatever I had to say, I found some comfort in him despite the general isolation and unfriendliness of life on the spaceship.

This guy was also probably a little excited over someone showing an interest in understanding the work that he did. He and I would sit in the "dead zones" of the ship, away from the eyes and ears of others (his one true talent was his unsurpassed ability to find such spaces), and talk in words the other was not going to understand but would unconditionally and uncritically accept. If one thought about it, what else was there in a friendship?

And once the topic of our conversation moved on to our pasts on Earth, especially our childhoods, our conversations became even more enriched. Thinking back, it was somewhat surprising; this guy was around the same age as me, but our countries, childhoods, and families were totally different. My father had been a military officer but not of some grand rank, and my family could not afford to send me to college, which was why I ended up joining the military and climbing the ranks to where I was now. This guy, on the other hand, had a mother who was a lawyer and a high-ranking government-official father—part of the elite class, in other words—and was pressured from an early age to take the bar or enter politics, but he had managed to stave them off and entered engineering school trusting only his crafty hands and sense of curiosity, whereupon he was practically disowned. Even when he made the national space agency in his country, meaning he had competed against and come out on top among the best mechanics of his country, his father was furious that he had made it as a "grease monkey" and not in a "proper" position like an administrator. The more I heard about his life, the less I could imagine it. My life, to him, was likely as incomprehensible.

Despite the way he was brought up, or perhaps because of it, there was a romantic streak to him that I could not understand. That was the only part of our conversations where there was friction. For example, to summarize his idea of our situation regarding the Disease, his hope was "to encounter an alien civilization much more advanced than ours, get a cure or treatment method from them, and save the world." While our unspoken rule was to accept whatever the other was saying unconditionally, that was the one thing I truly could not take seriously. But no matter what I said to counter his belief, he simply dug in his heels. I knew, from my regular communication with Earth, how aimlessly we were adrift in space and how desperate we were becoming, so my only friend on the ship being so clueless was extra depressing. Fearing this could lead into an argument or, worse, my letting slip confidential information by mistake, I always chose the safest path of giving up on convincing him.

I didn't know at the time, but he and I were not the only ones having grand debates on whether there was a cure for the

Disease or hope for humanity. The ship's passengers, who had displayed good camaraderie under our common goal of saving the world, were soon growing more and more exhausted; the doctors and scientists, the captain and technicians, they were all becoming ever more weary of spaceship life.

And then, finally, the Disease came on board.

There really is no such thing as discussion. We can give it fancier words like "negotiation" or "calibrating expectations" and such, but in the end, it's just one side that wins and the other has to give in. Even when both sides agree to compromise, there is always a side that compromises more than the other. Which makes one think that "compromise" is not a thing that really exists, either. All discussions and all negotiations are wars, and the result is always that one side ends up being the intimidating, violent side. This is especially true when the other side stubbornly insists on a perspective that one cannot compromise to. If the other side asks for an arm or a leg, or some other part of the body that can't be regenerated, the only reasonable thing to do is refuse.

The first person afflicted on board, the first helmsman, at a late hour in the night shift, calmly asked everyone but the second helmsman to leave the bridge. The other crew on the bridge thought it strange but nothing too out of the ordinary as they complied with the order, because his attitude and tone seemed very normal. Then the first helmsman locked the bridge hatch from the inside, casually approached the second helmsman, knocked him out with the wrench he was holding, and tucked into him, starting with the neck.

Whether it was by intention or an accident, all of the communication devices inside the bridge were not working, but there was still a CCTV feed that conveyed what was going on in the bridge in silent, high-resolution video. Most of the people screamed upon seeing it or closed their eyes or threw up, but some of the people peering into the monitors gazed at the first helmsman for a while and then picked up some heavy object in their vicinity and lunged at whoever was nearest to them. While most of the flight crew were distracted as they crowded in front of the bridge, trying desperately to open the airlock, the other cannibals were able to move through the ship without much hindrance and slowly, silently increase the death count. When the captain, only too late, realized there were other afflicted researchers and crew, she sent a team to take them out, who were mostly successful aside from a couple of afflicted who managed to escape and hide in the bowels of the ship. One of the escapees was the first mate.

It took approximately sixty-eight hours for the first helmsman to eat the other helmsman down to the skeleton. Then, seven hours later, he opened the bridge hatch, stepped out, and asked if he could have a sip of water. Crewmembers in pneumatic spacesuits seized him and locked him in the bridge.

It is very important to mention the time that had elapsed since the beginning of this situation—because the first helmsman had, from right before the moment he killed the second helmsman, engaged full warp.

So, the thing about this spaceship was that—being meant solely for escape—it wasn't designed to be shuttled from one fixed point to another within a given amount of time. Our priority was more about maintaining communications with Earth, and also to be able to return in the miraculous event that the Disease suddenly disappeared or a cure was found, and as such we had not been too far from our home planet. I suppose our ultimate goal was to return to Earth. The warp drive was there as an extra option, only to be used in extreme circumstances; only those who had the authorization to do so could activate it, but because we had never expected to use it, there were only four people who had this authorization: the captain, the first mate, the first helmsman, and the second helmsman. We needed the captain's command, two people among the four to type in their code, and two keys at the designated spots turned simultaneously, after which a handprint was required. Neglecting just one step out of the three could scuttle activation or fail to stop an activated drive.

The second helmsman was a skeleton with no handprint available at that point, and the first mate was both afflicted and AWOL, which meant the only people who could stop the drive was the captain and the first helmsman. But the first helmsman only demanded water and refused to cooperate with any other demand. When the captain commanded her crew to force the first helmsman to the bridge, they balked, citing the danger of infection, and there was a short argument. When the crew finally went to the brig to fetch the first helmsman, he had already eaten his left hand from the wrist down and was halfway through eating his right hand. As he licked the blood coming out of his left wrist as if it were a scrumptious ice-cream cone, he gave a bloody smile at the crew who had come to get him. The man was immediately moved to the infirmary and tied to a bed, but he soon died of massive hemorrhaging. They amputated his right hand and tried it on the scanner, but because half of it was gone, all they got was an error.

As this was going on, the spaceship continued top speed on a course that went on into infinite space, toward who knew what coordinates. To recap, two out of the four people who could use the conventional way of taking us out of warp were dead, one had disappeared, and the ones who were dead would perhaps still have helped if their hands hadn't been eaten. The unconventional way of deactivating the warp drive involved stopping all other systems in the spaceship. Of course, stopping a ship going at faster-than-light speeds would wreak havoc on the structural integrity of the ship—even a space ignoramus like me could foresee that, which meant there was vociferous debate among the passengers as to how to proceed. But there was no other alternative. After a few other weird alternatives were proposed, the discussion focused on attempting a full systems shutdown, with passengers and crew coming down on either side of the debate.

I was not a part of either side. Because I already knew there was no point in debate. From the moment the events on the bridge began, I was informing Earth of our situation, as per captain's orders. Not that I expected anyone on Earth to present us with a suitable alternative. But as soon as I had conveyed the exact nature of what was going on in the spaceship, the control towers on Earth stopped communicating with us. I tried every three minutes to reestablish links, but to no avail.

I knew very well indeed what this implied. When the spaceship designed to escape the Disease had become compromised, Earth had decided to abandon us.

After the captain heard my report, she sat there, silent. I waited for a long time for her to talk before asking, "What shall I do, Captain?"

"... I suppose it's for the best."

"Excuse me, ma'am?"

She looked me dead in the eye.

"It'll all work out." She lifted her hands and rubbed her mouth. "Keep trying to make contact. Until they answer."

Then, she left for the conference room, to have another discussion about the emergency stop.

As the captain and crew sat down for their continued debate, the medical doctors and scientists, who had been excluded from the official decision-making process, were having their own heated discussions about what was to be done. The physicists, whose expertise had been so unrelated to the Disease that they'd felt excluded until now, took the crisis as an opportunity to be heard as much as possible. As they engaged in their endless debate, the other scientists such as the medical doctors and biologists, pathologists, genetic engineers, chemists, and pharmacologists simply sat with them, killing time. An internal medicine specialist then bit off the ear of the genetic engineer seated next to him.

With a scream from the genetic engineer, their meeting room descended into chaos. The people inside tried to escape, but the security staff had been monitoring them on CCTV, and upon determining there was an outbreak among the research crew, they had immediately locked all exits. (Ever since the incident with the first helmsman, new emergency protocols had been implemented.) Everyone who had been in the meeting banged on the doors from the inside and screamed, while the internal medicine specialist continued to rip away at the genetic engineer with his teeth.

A biologist pounding at the exit ran up to the internal medicine specialist and punched his face. The doctor fell back as the biologist rained down punches while the genetic engineer, barely escaped from his immediate fate, wrapped his ripped face with his hands and moaned. The doctors and scientists who had rushed to the door at the first sign of danger fell back on their professional training and administered aid to the genetic engineer or ran to the biologist and the internal medicine specialist to stop their fight. A pathologist struck the biologist with a chair, who fell to the ground, the pathologist kicking him. Which was when the internal medicine specialist lunged at the pathologist.

The people in the meeting hall soon fell into three groups: one aided the genetic engineer, who had stopped screaming and had entered a state of shock, while the second clung to the doors but also gave up screaming and pounding, opting for catatonia. The third featured the internal medicine specialist, biologist, pathologist, the people trying to stop them from fighting, and the ones attacking the internal medicine specialist—a vigorously active group.

The reason this state of bedlam came to a pause was because one of the doctors taking care of the injured genetic engineer took a bite out of the genetic engineer's neck. A blood geyser gushed from his artery, splashing the people around him with lukewarm carmine, making them fall back. The people fighting also stopped their fisticuffs.

This was when the internal medicine specialist, beaten to a

pulp by then, leaped up and ran to the genetic engineer to rip at him. The genetic engineer convulsed as the internal medicine specialist ate him from his side. The biologist lunged at the internal medicine specialist and took an unexpected bite into the back of his neck.

Now it would be impossible to determine who was infected and who was not. Nor was it obvious who was still in their right minds and who had lost theirs; just because one was infected, it didn't mean they would show obvious signs of psychosis. If anything, the uninfected were more in danger of "psychosis" from the shock of what was happening. But ship security was not concerned with these little details, opting to keep the hatches locked.

Of the doctors and scientists on board, about two thirds died in this incident. This was about half the number of passengers and crew combined.

It took another 124 hours to confirm that everyone in that room was dead. During those five days, both the people ripping away at each other and the people watching them on the monitor had slowly lost their minds.

Hope for survival no longer had any meaning whatsoever.

That meeting room was permanently sealed off. I took a look at the security monitor from time to time and continued to summarize and transmit the situation to the control towers and my country's government authority on Earth, staring at the comms screen and waiting for a reply that never came. Then, I would slip down into the bottom of the hull.

This guy called it the "belly" of the ship, like the spaceship wasn't a machine but some large whale. Deep down in the belly as we leaned on nests of pipes and wires, this guy told me a story about a man who had allowed himself to be swallowed by a whale, by the will of God, and had survived.

"The will of God? You believe in that sort of thing?" I asked incredulously.

This guy was, however, as serious as always.

"I'm not talking about a one and true god that's similar to humans and has a human personality. If we could understand that god so well, they wouldn't be a god in the first place. But I believe there is something that's grander than what we can perceive with our five senses or comprehend with our human minds."

He timidly looked me in the eye.

"You're not going to tell me you don't believe it, too, are you? Not after coming out into space and encountering this vastness day and night? How could you not believe in a higher being after all this?"

My thoughts regarding this matter were completely different from his. Therefore, the best I could do was simply look disconcerted, shrug, and keep my mouth shut.

There was an awkward silence. Just when I was worried about having offended him, he said, "What's the situation up there like?"

"Not good." That's all I said.

He thought for a moment and asked again, "Can't you be more specific?"

"I just don't want to talk about it." I turned my head away from him. "There's no hope. ... None."

He seemed to think a bit more. Then he blurted, "You know,

I don't think hope is something that fundamentally exists or doesn't exist."

Now what was he talking about? When I didn't respond to him, he murmured, "A Chinese writer once said that in a story." Then, after a pause, "It was a story about going back home."

"You read Chinese literature?"

"Of course," he replied proudly, "I study a lot."

To me, "study" meant reading research papers or writing them. Reading stories was not studying. But following our unspoken rule, I simply nodded.

"Hope," he went on, "exists simply because we happen to think it. Space is vast, but even so, there are laws that govern every star, planet, and satellite. There must be a reason we made it this far, a purpose. All we need to do now is to fulfill that purpose."

Listening to this guy made me think of a joke one of the doctors had made when our ship set forth: "All we need to do now is find a cure for the Disease." How empty, meaningless, sorrowful.

"Someday, I know for sure, we'll return home. We'll go back to Earth and save humanity, restore hope. Because hope is something that only needs to be thought into being."

He gave me a playful punch to the arm.

Clearly he did not "study" enough. I didn't bother explaining to him that the Chinese writer's story in question involved a main character who returns home and experiences only tragedy and despair.

Then, the captain appeared.

She emerged from the shadows as if conjured out of the darkness. This guy and I quickly got to our feet, him bumping his head on an overhead pipe in the process. As he gave a yelp and rubbed his head, the captain reflexively extended a hand toward him.

"Are you all right? Did I surprise you?"

"No … no, ma'am."

The captain took a hold of his head by his temples and tilted his head. Not sure of how to react, this guy simply followed along with the captain's manipulations.

"Let's see … I really think you should head to the infirmary."

"Oh no, I'm fine, ma'am."

The captain grinned somewhat mischievously at this guy's perturbed face. "Are you worried about being caught dawdling during work hours?"

I hastily butted in, "We're not in work hours, ma'am, we're off shift."

The captain let go of his head.

"There's an ongoing emergency situation, it just won't do not to be accounted for, even if you're off shift. Have you both received permission from your superiors to come down here and loiter around like this?"

I didn't know about this guy, but she was right about me. My superior was the captain, and I'd never asked for her permission to go hide in the underbelly of the spaceship.

"I'm sorry, Captain."

"Never mind that. Don't get caught next time."

And just as swiftly as she had appeared, she vanished into the darkness.

What had happened seemed so unreal that this guy and I stood side by side in silence. Until I murmured, "How did the captain know we were here?"

This guy didn't answer. He had one hand on his temple and was looking down.

"What's wrong? Does it hurt a lot?"

He didn't answer. Still with his hand on his head, he began to walk away.

"Where are you going?" I asked, puzzled. "What's wrong? What happened?" He didn't answer and simply widened his stride, feeling his way with his free hand along the pipes running by us as I went after him. Then, he stopped. Not lowering his hand, he unclipped the torch on his utility belt and shone its light around in front of him.

"What's going on? What?"

I finally caught up to him, grabbed his shoulder, and turned him around. The light of his torch shone in my eyes, but it was his face that made me flinch.

"Blood!" I said. "Did you hit your head that hard? Come on, let's go to the infirm—"

"It's not mine."

His expression was almost blank as he looked into my eyes, his voice on the edge of cracking.

"What?"

"It's not my blood."

Then, he turned and shone a spot ahead of us.

There, illuminated by his powerful torch, cheek ripped out and chunks of flesh missing in the torso and stomach, was the body of the first mate.

Who had been infected first, the captain or the first mate? Or had the first mate never been infected in the first place, and it had just been the captain all along? I kept thinking these now-useless thoughts as I looked down at the corpse that had once been the first mate. This guy, while shining his light down on the scene, didn't dare approach the body either.

"I've never seen a dead body before ..."

I didn't know what to say to that.

Instead, I said, "The right hand is missing."

"What?"

"The body is missing its right hand."

I suppose in moments of danger, the synapses of our brains also start firing at warp speed. Not that there's a way of verifying whether the thoughts obtained at warp were right or useful. The first mate's right hand hadn't been eaten; it had been sliced off at the wrist. I suddenly remembered the captain's reaction when I had reported our communications with Earth had been severed; "I suppose it's for the best," she had said, raising her hand to cover what I finally realized was a smile.

As long as she had the first mate's hand, whether it's the right one or left one, the captain could activate and deactivate the warp drive at will. She could take the ship anywhere in space. As long as the ship contained survivors, she would have plenty of food on board. She had never cared about what happened on Earth to begin with.

I said, "We have to crash-land the ship."

"What?"

"We have to stop the warp drive! It doesn't matter where we crash, as long as we crash! We have to get off this ship!"

"What are you talking about? Why do we need to crash the ship? We need to go back to—"

"We can't go back to Earth!" I said cutting in. "If we stay on this ship, *we all die*. We have to get out of here by any means necessary."

"Are you crazy!"

He was about to say more but I shouted him down.

"You saw it, too! The captain is infected. We're just food to her. Do you think she's going to let us cure the Disease? Do you think she's really going to let us all go back to Earth!"

This guy didn't say anything to that.

"Look," I said, "do you know how to stop the warp drive? Do you know how to land this thing?"

He shook his head. "I can't do it on my own."

I tried to speak calmly, but my voice unintentionally went up to a scream. "*Then we need to gather more people! All the people who aren't infected yet—*"

"How are we going to tell who is infected and who isn't?" His voice was actually calming, as if he were speaking to an agitated child. "You saw the captain. Did you have the slightest inkling she was infected until you saw the blood on my face?"

I had nothing to say.

"There's a lifeboat," he said, quietly but firmly. "We're getting out of here."

I hadn't even thought of lifeboats. Who knew such things existed on spaceships? This ship, after all, was in itself a lifeboat from Earth. Did lifeboats need lifeboats?

In any case, every plan comes with a catch.

"There's exactly one," he said quickly, "and we can't get to it now."

"Why? I mean, why not?" My speech was also picking up speed.

"We're in warp. The access hatch won't open."

I felt my body go limp.

He was also silent for a moment. Then he looked up at me and said, "Let's try for an emergency stop."

"How?"

"I don't know exactly myself. But I heard that at least the first mate and captain have the power to bring warp to an emergency stop. I'll try to find out more."

Seeing my expression, he gave my shoulder another friendly jab.

"Go back for now. We've been down here too long. I'll contact you once I find something."

As he turned to leave, my brain, with some difficulty, started functioning again.

"How are you going to bypass a first-mate authorization?"

"I don't know," he said, looking back at me. "I figure something will come up once I put my mind to it."

This guy grinned. Then, he turned, and like the captain before him, disappeared into the dark.

Making my way back to the upper levels, I thought to myself that it was probably faster for me to look into the problem of authorization.

Not that it would be easier for me, necessarily, to find what we needed to know. But it was true I was often in the captain's ready room and would not arouse suspicion if I happened to be caught in it. Now that I knew her status I felt apprehensive about entering her ready room, but seeing as I felt no desire to eat anyone, I thought it was reasonable to assume I was not infected.

But even if I could slip into the ready room, what, exactly, would I be looking for inside? I knew her serial number, but there had to be more to it than that. What more did I need to find?

I called this guy.

"I don't know either. All I know is, it can only be done from the bridge."

"The bridge?"

That was even more dangerous than the ready room. It was, along with the scientists' meeting room, the last place I wanted to visit on this ship.

"There's really no way to do it anywhere else?"

"Only the bridge. As far as I know."

I hung up and got off the elevator. Slowly walking down the long corridor to my quarters, I was lost in thought.

I came into my quarters. I sat in front of the computer. I stared into the screen.

Salvation doesn't come to those who just wait.

I got up.

I went to get a spacesuit.

Within the airtight spacesuit, I not so much as walked but lightly bounced down the dark corridor to the bridge, so nervous I was gulping dry air.

Both the bridge and the scientists' meeting room were on the top level of the ship, which was now entirely blocked off. There was no electricity, life support, or artificial gravity there. The pitch dark made the corridors seem longer the farther I went. My weak torchlight revealed the occasional patch of ice on the walls.

I was at the bridge hatch. A cross of biohazard warning tape was stuck on it and the hatch itself was sealed. I wasn't sure if an alarm would sound the moment I tried to open the hatch.

But as I approached, I saw that while the tape was intact, the hatch behind it was, in fact, half-open.

I couldn't believe it; I stared. I reached over and pushed the hatch. It swung open.

After a moment of hesitation, I entered the open hatch.

The bridge, like the corridors, was dark. I switched on my torch again.

The light blinded me for a moment. I could just about make out the controls, but I had no idea what any of them did. The splatters of blood from floor to ceiling made me feel dizzy.

This was a mistake. Should I call this guy again? If I showed him the bridge through the camera of my comm device, would he find the emergency stop for me?

The gauntlet of my spacesuit was so bulky that there was no way I could grip my device. The more buttons I pushed, the more mistakes I made, and the more anxious I got.

That was when I heard a sound.

I stopped what I was doing. I listened.

Was it coming from me? I wasn't used to the spacesuit after all.

When I started struggling with my comms again, I heard

rustling from another corner—a monitor somewhere in the room was activated.

WHO IS IT? The screamed words formed in my head but my voice refused to form the words. Instead, my body reflexively turned to the direction of the rustling, the beam of my torch swinging around.

The distance was far, and the torch weak. The beam couldn't quite make it all the way there. But the dim light of the monitor across the bridge was falling on someone's face.

The first mate's profile was only lit in outline, with the rest of his features in shadow. But even in that shadow I could see his left cheek was eaten away. Through that hole I could see the bloody ivory of his teeth and jawbone.

With just the remaining half of his face, the first mate grinned. Then, as if saying hello, he lifted his left hand.

When the first mate placed his dead hand on the lit screen, all the functions of the spaceship came to a stop.

Aside from the great shock, I don't remember much.

There was shaking. Not just a couple of shakes but like pills being shaken in a pill container. I think I briefly lost consciousness for a bit. I don't know how many times I fainted, or how long it took me to come to. There were several flashes of light, and then utter darkness.

What I do remember is that whenever I came to, I kept looking around me in the bridge.

I was, of course, alone in there.

Maybe it was better to die like this than end up like the dead first mate. I could find no reason to be afraid or sad.

I have no idea how this guy managed to find me. I think he was trying to tell me something, but I could only see his lips move and could hear nothing. Once he had floated up to me and pulled me out of the bridge, he pulled out a rappelling hook with a retractable cable from my spacesuit and hooked it onto his. (I'd had no idea the spacesuits came with such a feature until that moment.) When he swam out of the bridge, I followed.

Many objects were floating beside us in the corridors. Darkness, fire, water, bodies, blood. Various fragments that were once part of a person's body.

There was only the spacesuit standing between me and certain death.

As we waded through hell, the fact that all this was actually happening to me was incredible.

I tugged at the cable linking me to this guy. He looked back.

"What happened?" I shouted. "How did you know I was at the bridge?"

This guy pointed to his wrist. I looked down at my gauntlet. There were several buttons of all shapes, but my brain refused to register any of the meanings behind them. He jerked the cable and I whooshed to his side. He pressed a button on my gauntlet.

—I was also going to the bridge.

His voice was like thunder in my ears.

—I was looking for the same thing as you.

And I was afraid for my eardrums. But he kept shouting, regardless.

—The ship might blow. We've got to go.

He turned and continued to swim down the corridor. I finally understood that he was grabbing safety rungs to propel himself forward. Doing the same, I followed.

I had a feeling, whenever we got to a door or a hatch, that it wouldn't open, but they invariably would without any hassle. The locks must've been disengaged when the ship's systems went down. This was one of the useless thoughts that floated through my head in my ongoing state of shock as I allowed myself to be led through the ship.

Countless corridors and doors—and bodies and body parts floating up to us at every turn. We were randomly drenched with water at one point. But these were relatively easy obstacles to overcome.

When we finally came to a door that wouldn't open, I thought we had at last come to the inevitable. But unlike me, who was immediately ready to give up, this guy grabbed the door and vigorously started to pull.

—Come on, pull with me! We've got to get it open!

This voice was ringing in my helmet.

Thankfully I found the goddamn volume control, otherwise my hearing would've been damaged beyond repair before getting off the damn ship. But there was no time to respond, ask, or convey my thoughts to him anyway. I got on the opposite sliding door and started to pull. There was no gravity, which made it difficult to fix my body in a certain direction and concentrate my strength.

The door started to shake a little. This guy looked up at me. I pulled harder.

He whipped himself around, jerking me along because of

the cable that connected us, and started walking off rapidly as he muttered:

—That was the faster route, the shortcut. ... This way will take longer. ... How much time do we have before it explodes? ... Oxygen running out in these suits. ... We have to go, go, go ...

It must be true that in a crisis situation, we tap into superhuman powers. How he could move so adeptly without having gravity to move against is something I would've marveled at if I had room in my mind to marvel at anything at that moment. As I was dragged along by the cable, I gave up on matching his pace and tried to preserve some remnant of dignity by trying to keep myself right side up as we made our way through the corridors, straining with all my might not to flip over on my tether.

Then, a sudden stop. With difficulty, I managed to right myself.

Before I could ask him what was wrong, the light of a torch shined right into my eyes.

And over the shoulder of this guy in front of me, I saw the face of the captain.

She was not alone. There were about five or six crewmembers surrounding her. They were all injured and bleeding in places.

Probably the last survivors.

Probably all infected ...

The captain took a step toward us. Her torchlight hit my retinas again; I winced and shielded my eyes.

Through the ghostlike afterimage her light had left, I could see the captain's lips move. Not that I could hear anything she was saying. Neither she nor the other crew members were wearing spacesuits.

This guy's voice cut through my thoughts over the comm:

—What shall we do?

"Do what?"

—The captain, you know she's infected. We can't take her on the escape pod.

His head turned toward me.

—You're a soldier. Do something.

He wanted me to do something to the captain? Like, a one-person mutiny? Not that words like "mutiny" had any meaning under these circumstances. I carefully tapped the side of my spacesuit. Normally, I did not carry a loaded gun on board the ship, but when I had decided to make my way to the sealed bridge, I had prepared it just in case.

My gauntlet touched the side of my spacesuit. It was then I realized.

I had taken the gun out of my drawer and holstered it to my belt, *and then* I had gotten the spacesuit.

The gun was underneath my spacesuit.

How could I have made such a stupid mistake in this situation … I couldn't believe it.

I untethered myself from this guy and took a step forward. My gaze casually drifted to my left gauntlet where this guy had pressed my buttons. Suddenly, the transmission button came into view. I pressed it. I spoke as calmly as I can, as if my life depended on it, because it did:

"Ma'am, we cannot go down the corridor back there."

It wasn't clear whether the captain could hear me, but I shouted it nonetheless:

"There's a fire back there, ma'am. We have to go back the other way."

The captain said something. I shook my head.

"I can't hear you, ma'am."

She pressed a button somewhere on the shoulder of her uniform.

—What happened? Did someone execute the emergency stop? What are the casualties, the survivors?

"I don't know, ma'am."

It wasn't as if I could tell her that the first mate's half-eaten, reanimated corpse was trying to screw us all over.

"We came to determine that very thing, but I believe we are the only survivors at this time."

—And the damage to the ship?

—Critical.

That last part was from this guy, who butted in. Apparently, he had regained his wits.

The captain nodded.

—Do you two know about the lifeboat?

Of course the captain of all people would know about the lifeboat—but the word "lifeboat" coming out of an infected person made my vision go dark.

—We must go further down to the hull and look for more survivors.

—How could you, as the captain, even think about abandoning ship!

It was this guy butting in again. I wanted to stop him but he didn't give me an inch to do so.

—You want us to run away? How could you say such a thing? You were supposed to do something when we caught the first infections!

A crewmember roused himself from his stupor:

—What's the meaning of this? How dare you speak this way to the captain!

—What captain! She's infected! This was her plan all along! To steal the ship with her helmsman so she could take us into space where they can eat all of us!

He was shouting now.

—What are you talking about?

The captain's expression was still dead calm, but her voice had taken an unsettling tone. This guy wasn't, however, in the mood to perceive such subtleties. He was screaming at the other crewmembers:

—Can't you see? The captain is infected! She's been infected for a long time! She killed the first mate and ate him! She's going to eat you all!

He kicked the wall and went flying. If I hadn't untethered myself, I would've gone flying, too.

—We can't give you the lifeboat! You're all infected! You're all going to die, all of you!

The crewmembers converged on him. Because gravity had been turned off, they were all clumsy, and it was easier said than done, even with so many of them grabbing at him at once—but this guy was also in a state of zero-gravity and could not get away that fast himself.

The captain didn't move. She dispassionately observed the crewmembers and this guy tumble around, not saying a word. Then, she unholstered her gun.

As soon as I saw her gun, I lunged at her.

The biggest problem the afflicted have working against them is the fact that they perceive all other people as food.

Food is something you eat or store away to consume at some other time, it is not your colleague. No one thinks of working together with their food to overcome some untenable situation.

Everyone was attacking this guy, but the lack of gravity and his spacesuit was slowing him down. On the other hand, his spacesuit gave him a level of protection that let him fend them off, plus a few of the crewmembers were now attacking each other.

The captain was much more adept at moving in zero-G than I was. My training kicked in as I tried to disarm her, but the lack of gravity and the presence of my spacesuit made it impossible to strike at her hand holding the gun. Though, come to think of it, I never did receive any training for a zero-G situation. Our fight had devolved into an ineffectual bodily struggle between the two of us.

Suddenly, I saw the point of her gun pointing right at me. As soon as that little black hole came into view I wondered whether my spacesuit was rayproof (it probably wasn't) and would she eat me afterward, and would I come back to half-life like the first mate if she did—all of that rushed through my mind in less than a second.

Who knows how I twisted the captain's wrist in what direction. The gun fired, and the ray sliced through her stomach and burned the leg of a crewmember that was taking a bite out of the neck of another crewmember.

Looking bewildered, the captain looked down at her stomach. I freed myself from her grasp and grabbed the gun that was adrift in the air; just as the captain turned to face me, I aimed at her forehead and fired.

This guy had formed a tumbleweed with the other crewmembers. I really didn't want to kill any more people, but because they were trying to take my spacesuit off at this point, I had to shoot a few more of them.

This time it was me who was dragging him through the spaceship, with him being half out of his mind.

No one got in our way now. I don't know how many corridors we passed and turns we made before coming up to a large and black airlock.

Nervous, I glanced at this guy. But before I could say anything, he went right up to a little red light by the hatch and took off one of his gauntlets.

He keyed in a seven-digit code and placed his palm on the wall scanner. The airlock slid upward.

It was complete darkness inside—nothing was visible. But when the airlock had opened to human height, the lights came on. This guy said:

—Get in.

The term "lifeboat" had made me think it was some kind of tiny escape pod, but while it was indeed small, it was actually a full-fledged spacecraft that had everything a spacefaring vessel required.

Once we were inside and the airlock was sealed, I untethered myself from him again. I was about to take off my helmet when he stopped me. He strode into the lifeboat and I followed.

The helm lit up, and so did the central illumination. This guy disengaged the docking link. The outer hatch of the mothership opened. Much quieter and gentler than I expected, the lifeboat drifted out and away from the ship into an endlessly dark space.

Only when this guy took off his helmet and spacesuit did I take mine off, too.

We sat at the helm and said nothing as we looked out at the mothership shrinking in the distance, becoming part of the darkness of space.

Impossible then to put my finger on why, but it seemed like a logical ending.

I asked this guy where we were going.

"We're going back," he said as if it were obvious.

I'd expected this answer, but hearing him say it was demoralizing.

"We don't have a warp drive like the mothership does, but the distance to Earth is—"

"We can't go there," I said. "There's nothing on Earth."

He stared at me for a moment before asking, "How do you know that?"

This time, it was me who took a moment.

Not that there was any good reason to hesitate; I was simply trained to be discreet. But how ridiculous was it that I would even care about confidentiality and operations security at this point?

So I just told him.

"My job was to keep us in contact with Earth. And as soon as I reported that the Disease was on board the ship, they abandoned us."

"What?"

"They ceased all contact with us."

He didn't say a word.

I looked him in the eye. "Following the captain's orders, I tried to reestablish contact every three minutes, but there was no answer whatsoever. They abandoned us. And now that we've come this far on warp, there's no way we could determine what the situation is like on Earth."

"But they could've found a cure for the Disease by now, or maybe it's gone away?"

The strength of his optimism was almost admirable in light of the disaster we had found ourselves in.

"There's hardly any probability of something like that. And more than that ..." I gestured at the blackness of space outside, "it's more likely that what happened on the mothership happened on Earth by now."

We sat in silence for another moment before he spoke again.

"Do you really think so?"

I nodded.

"Then what are we supposed to do?"

"Land somewhere." I thought a bit more. "Somewhere similar to Earth's environment."

He said nothing as he stared at the floor. Then, he turned and looked into the navigation screen. Initializing it with a touch of his palm, he started calculating something.

After a long while, he spoke again.

"I got it. The coordinates are in. But we have to sleep to get there."

"Sleep?"

He looked at me for a moment and spoke slowly. "I told you. This ship has no warp. There are no planets within a few hundred light-years with environments suitable for human habitation. Riding it out like this is going to lead us to age to death in this lifeboat."

He pressed something in the corner of the screen and looked back. I turned to look at what he was looking at. A door slid open behind the cockpit, and I could see hibernation capsules.

"Once we reach a habitable planet, the computer will wake us."

"We're going to wander until then without a clear destination?"

He frowned. "What other choice do we have? Space isn't a highway. There are no billboards, no control towers telling us what to do."

He was right. But I was still hesitant.

"What's the nearest planet? Shouldn't we know that at least before we go into hibernation?"

"The atmosphere of the closest planet has no hydrogen or oxygen and is nine hundred degrees by day and below freezing by night. You want us to land there?"

I felt depressed.

"What's the nearest after that? One where at least the temperatures—"

"Like I said, the computer will wake us when we find a place like that. Look," he said in a placating tone, "machines like this are my specialty. I've programmed it so they'll let us know as soon as they find a habitable planet. We'll never find a place with the exact atmospheric profile, but at the very least, it'll be a place we can walk around without spacesuits. But planets like that aren't exactly a dime a dozen. If you're so suspicious, see for yourself."

I looked back at the helm. The search query and the result "o" were just about discernable, but the rest was gibberish to me.

"All right, fine," I said. "But we can't go back to Earth. There is really no hope there."

"I know, I know." He stood up. "You go in first. I'll switch it to autopilot and make one more general inspection before turning in."

Reluctantly, I nodded.

Cryogenic sleep was a new one for me. He took me into the capsule and tucked me into the harness like he was putting a child to sleep. Right before the canopy closed, he patted my head.

"Sweet dreams."

Before I could answer him, the canopy shut.

And when I woke up, we were back on Earth.

I realized I'd been fooled when we were minutes away from entering Earth's atmosphere. My cryogenic hangover was fierce, and I was having trouble breathing. My body felt like it had gone through a wringer and every movement was an effort. This guy dragged me to the helm.

"We're back home."

Despite his confession, it took a few more minutes of staring out the window to realize what was happening. An electronic voice warned that we were seven minutes away from atmospheric entry.

"What have you done?" My voice came out a scream, splitting in the end.

He was practically nonchalant.

"I just thought, what if we wandered the universe looking for a planet that was just like Earth and wandered into an asteroid belt? If we really needed an environment like Earth, we should just come to Earth. This is home, after all."

"No! This isn't home anymore. We can't land here!" I vigorously shook my head. "I don't know what's going to be down there, but it isn't the Earth we know. It's not home! We can't go back!"

"It's too late," he said as calmly as you please, "we're too far gone and need to land."

"What!"

Five minutes before landing.

"I suggest you sit down and grab on to something. Or go back into the capsule?"

"I can't die because you're in a sentimental mood, turn this ship around! We'll both die if we go back to Earth!"

"I said it's too late," he said with a smile.

I looked into his eyes. Convincing him seemed out of the question; should I fight? Did I have enough time to overpower him and prevent the landing? In any case, I had to prevent us from landing. Going back to that place was the one thing that I needed to stop at all costs.

He looked back at me and said, "What are you going to do? Can you fly this ship without me?"

He was right.

Two minutes to entry.

"Grab on to something," he said again.

I stood there looking at the screen and then back at him.

"Look," he said annoyed, "if you want to break your neck after coming all the way we came, do exactly that. You've been on a spaceship before, you know what's going to happen if you don't sit down."

I sighed. There was nothing to be done but comply. But as I strapped myself in, I had to say one more thing. "Just promise me this."

"What?"

"After we land, don't open the hatch or try to get out before we know the situation outside, all right? Even if there are survivors, they could be infected."

He thought for a moment and then nodded his head.

We entered the atmosphere.

It was considerably bumpy, but the landing was more or less a success. He even boasted a little about it not being bad considering it was his first landing attempt. I didn't care.

"Do not open the door, and do not try to go outside."

"All right, all right."

I glanced out the window as I checked the atmospheric content and our humidity, temperature, and signs of life. The air wasn't too different from when we had left, but there were absolutely no signs of life.

This guy looked a little disappointed.

"What happened? Humanity can't have been completely wiped off the face of the Earth."

"Not if we failed to eradicate the Disease. Even if there are survivors, I doubt they resemble anything near to what we would call 'humanity.'"

"Don't be such a downer," he snarled. "Look. I have to get out there."

"No, just no. It's stranger somehow that there are no signs of life at all. Let's wait a little more—"

He shouted, "We're here, what's there to wait for?"

In the silence that followed, a machine voice was heard.

—Signal detected. Receiving.

Rows of symbols lit up the console display.

—Receiving.

"Look," he said excitedly, "people! You were wrong, someone is still alive and sending out signals. There must be an enclave of people who survived the Disease."

I looked at the screen. Nothing he was saying was registering in my mind.

"What is it? What's the language? What is it saying?" he demanded.

I didn't answer.

What lit up the screen was pictograms and symbols. It wasn't a language, it was code. The moment I saw the first line, I didn't need to decode it to know what it said.

It was my code. Stating that the Disease had occurred in the spaceship and we required assistance.

He didn't believe me.

"There's no way."

"Why would I lie to you?"

"Because I lied to you."

Uh, what? "This isn't the time to get into some petty argument. What could I possibly gain from doing something like that?"

He didn't respond. Just as I was about to say something more, he opened his mouth.

"If you're right, and humanity has been destroyed because of the Disease, you and I are the only humans left in this universe."

I hadn't thought of it like that, but it was true.

"That's it, then."

"What's it?"

He slowly stood up.

"Even if humanity didn't survive, we're still together. And we got back home." He looked down at the floor. "We can start again. Like Adam and Eve."

"What are you saying?"

He raised his head and met my eyes. "Like I said before. Hope exists if you think it to existence. If you don't have any, you can just make it up. And we're here, together."

Slowly, he approached me.

"We can be each other's hope. We'll start everything from the beginning. We'll reconstruct humanity. Create new meanings. Us two."

An extended hand.

"Isn't this amazing?"

I did not like the look in his eyes.

What happens in the outside world has nothing to do with whether I hope for it or not. Just because I want things to go back the way they were, it doesn't mean they will; that's what I had tried to tell this guy all along.

Maybe hope exists just because we think it to existence, and meaning is something you create on your own. But that's just an individual's subjective experience of faith. There's no guarantee that such subjective faith will be supported by the objective situation. Why should the myriad ways of the universe conspire to realize the will of a mere individual?

I'm not trying to be cynical. I'm simply saying, by pointing out how small and insignificant I am, that whatever I do is also small and insignificant and makes no difference in this universe. There is no responsibility I need to take for the universe, and no duty for me to reconstruct humanity on my own. From a practical perspective, at least.

But coming back down to Earth—I may have been in a mere administrative post lately, but at the end of the day, I was a trained soldier while he was just a civilian. Aerospace mechanics do not receive such training.

To not consider these facts before leaping to attack me was, in the end, his ultimate mistake.

The sun hadn't set completely yet. But the sky was turning gray. The wind was getting colder. Warmth still clung onto the concrete lump I was sitting on, but it would grow completely cold soon.

Here I was, all alone on a ruined planet. There were many ways of accepting this fate, but for now, I was at peace. The world was ridiculous, and beautiful, and free.

The last vestige of warmth disappeared from the concrete. Trembling, I stood up.

I decided I should go back to the ship and finish eating this guy.

A Very Ordinary Marriage

My wife began making those phone calls just shy of our first wedding anniversary. Or perhaps—no, I'm sure of this now—it started before that. From right after we married, or even before we met. She must've been making those calls all along. I just didn't know. Because she never dropped the slightest hint of what she was doing behind my back.

Was I dim, or had she been that cautious? At what point is a husband supposed to become aware that his wife is making suspicious phone calls? The marital advice discussion boards that I once spent hours on online were full of such stories. *My wife keeps calling someone. My wife keeps messaging someone. She put a passcode on her phone for the first time. It's been three months. It's been going on a week.* Some of these husbands went a year, two years, even five without realizing a single thing.

Was it *normal* not to have suspected anything for such a long time, if I'd been an ordinary husband?

"Honey?" It's my wife, in the bedroom. "What are you doing?"

"Smoking. I'm only having one."

"All right." Then, after a moment of silence, she adds, "I wish you'd quit."

So that's today's version. She has a set catalog of responses. I wish you'd quit. Or: Close the door, you're making the room smell. Or: The downstairs neighbors will complain.

I answer, "All right. Just one."

After, I think about how this is the normal answer to this complaint. It's what most husbands would say in this situation.

And then, I think of my wife's hands.

Jiyoung and I met at a dentist's waiting room. I was there because I had serious toothache, and Jiyoung was in the middle of straightening her teeth.

I was sitting there, waiting for my turn and looking at my phone as if there were anything interesting there, when Jiyoung walked out of the orthodontist's room. Of course, I didn't know she was Jiyoung then. She was small, more the cute type than pretty. Her earnest expression as she listened intently to the nurse made her look even cuter than at first glance.

It was all acting, of course, but her expression seemed so sincere. Jiyoung was the kind of person who was sincere in everything she did, someone who always tried to do her best, to the point of overdoing it a little.

I hesitated for a long time over making a move. She didn't always have an appointment when I did, and there were days when my session would be over and the cute little lady would be nowhere in sight. Like the day of my final session.

I felt regret. More regret than I'd expected.

Which was why, when I bumped into her in the middle of the street on the way to the hypermarket, I inadvertently made such a joyful fuss.

"Hey—hey! It's you!"

I was shouting and pointing to her as she gazed over the store windows, slowly walking in my direction.

"It's you, isn't it? From the dentist! You know, Barunmiso Dentistry!"

I yelled this so loudly that she gave a start, stopped in her tracks, and looked at me. Not just her, but everyone passing by.

Mortification. What was I doing? When did I become the type of man who came on to women I didn't know? I was quite the opposite, in fact. The kind who would judge other men who would brag about "hunting" a woman on the street or getting the phone number of some woman who worked at a subcontractor.

But the sight of her with her eyes open wide and slightly afraid as she stared back at me was even cuter than her serious face. Who knew why I was doing such a thing, but there she was, looking at me with her big brown eyes full of questions. Well, if I'd drawn my sword, I had to at least slice a head of cabbage before putting it back in the sheath.

Or was it turnip, not cabbage? What was that saying?

"Don't you know me? You've seen me in the dentist's waiting room. Do you live around here?"

"What? Oh, yes ..."

Her voice trailed off. Her eyes were still wide, and she was beginning to look uneasy. I had to do something, but I didn't know what exactly.

"Are you finished with the orthodontist? You weren't there the last time I was there. I'm all done up. I had to redo a cavity, and my dentist said I might as well redo all of my cavities because amalgams just don't last that long. He showed me an X-ray, too ..."

The more I rambled on, the longer her eyes remained wide and the more embarrassed and disconcerted she seemed. I quickly took out my wallet, found a business card, and held it out to her.

"This is my card, please call me."

Aside from the sheer lack of reason for her to do so, my gesture was done with such alacrity that I would kick myself later, but I couldn't think of anything else in that moment. Having presented her with my business card as if it were the decapitated head of her greatest enemy, she took a step back as if she were being mugged.

Dammit. She was never going to take the card.

She took the card.

She mumbled something I couldn't hear, bowed her head a little, and quickly walked away. I stood in front of the cosmetics store like an idiot and watched her disappear down the subway entrance.

Because *that* was our first meeting—or our first conversation, rather—I was sure she would never call me. I tried to forget any of it ever happened. When she did call, it was a number I didn't know so I didn't even pick up. Hours later, when I called back just in case, it turned out to be her.

"So ... why did you give me your business card again?"

That was why she had called me.

Which was why, when she became my wife two years later, I thought: *Miracles really do happen.*

I remember almost nothing from the wedding whatsoever. Just one thing. The moment I put a wedding ring on her finger.

Her left hand on mine was very, very small. So small and

fragile compared to mine, and a little cold, perhaps because she was nervous. For a second I forgot about the ceremony and wanted to rub her hands warm like I normally do.

The touch of that little, slender, soft ring finger, my silent promise to her that I would spend my life keeping those hands warm—I remember all of that. I will never forget that moment for as long as I live.

I try, now, to remember her hands, to remember that moment as much as I can.

I breathe deeply.

The cigarette that I haven't taken a drag from is almost burned down to a stub. I quickly bring it to my lips.

Because I'm here on the balcony for a smoke, aren't I? Because isn't that what I told my wife?

Because an ordinary husband doesn't come out to the balcony for a smoke and then just hold the cigarette in his hand.

Because I'm an ordinary husband who smokes on the balcony.

Thinking back, I do seem to recall seeing my wife calling someone all the time, right after we got married. I just didn't pay much attention.

My wife made a lot of phone calls. To my mother, my younger sister, daily calls, even, to my sister. She asked after them, listened to their boring stories as if she were fascinated. My mother and sister adored her for that. Which is why I didn't think too much about the great number of calls she made. Women like to talk on the phone, and my wife was a socially outgoing person, that's her personality, so what.

It would've been wonderful if we could've continued to live that way. The *so what* way.

I do not know the exact time my wife began those particular calls, but my sense that there was something strange was aroused a little less than a year after our wedding.

On that summer evening, I was feeling unwell after a night out drinking with my colleagues. It wasn't as if it was my first time, and I was a pretty good drinker, but it was a restaurant I had never gone to before and there must've been something in the food. I had come home and lay down in bed to go to sleep when half an hour later I was running to the bathroom to throw up.

It didn't end once I'd thrown up everything in my stomach; I kept heaving and heaving. Even when there was nothing that could possibly be in there anymore. After much dry heaving and clutching the rim of the toilet, I managed to eventually crawl out the bathroom door. My wife was going to have to take me to the hospital, she had to get me to the emergency room ...

But she wasn't standing outside the bathroom. Nor was she on the bed. I lay on the threshold between the bathroom and master bedroom and waited for her in vain. Like some stout, thick snake, I crawled across the bedroom floor to the living room.

My insides felt like they would burst, and I kept dry heaving, which made that short distance, otherwise traversable in a few steps, a vast desert. When I finally reached the living room door, which was ajar, I still didn't have the strength to stand up on my own, so I nudged open the door a bit wider and stuck my head out the gap.

My wife was in the living room. "Jiyoung-ah ..." I called out her name, but there was so little strength in my voice that my wife didn't hear me. I realized she was on the phone.

She's calling the ambulance, was the first thought that crossed my mind. *I don't think it's as serious as that,* was the next, although I did feel grateful. What if they carted me over there and it turned out to be just drunken throwing up? I thought of how embarrassing that would be.

But upon a closer listen, my wife was not calling an ambulance. Nor was she calling her parents or mine. She was speaking in a language I had never heard before. Sounds I never would've imagined were coming out of her mouth. Even as I think back now, it's as clear as a movie scene for me.

I was in too much pain to think much about it at the time. My voice failed me once more. Straining, I pushed the door in front of me as hard as possible and it slammed against the wall. My wife gave a start, and looked over.

Jiyoung-ah, I mouthed at her. She came running.

Hospital, I mouthed again. She sat next to me and stroked my hair like I was a child.

"I've called the ambulance," she said.

And a little while later, the ambulance came.

I decided to forget about that phone call.

It was only for one night, but I'd never in my life had to stay in a hospital before. Not to mention get an IV drip hooked into me. Who knows what was in that thing, but lying there with the drip made me feel less like I was about to die by the minute.

The whole time, my wife sat right by me. The only time she wasn't there was when she went to the reception desk to get me admitted.

But there was one moment, when I fell dead asleep and woke up at dawn, when I felt like she was definitely not there. I don't know if she'd gone to the bathroom or was making a phone call or what. But in my half-woke state, I felt like my wife was nowhere in this hospital, that she had left me behind while I was sleeping. I fell into a panic.

There wasn't an ounce of strength in me to get up and look for her; from my lying-down position, I tried to find my phone. But my body refused to listen to me. I listlessly clawed at the air and the bedsheet with my fingers and dropped into a deep sleep once more.

The next day was a Saturday, so I stayed in. I'd come home from the hospital and tried to get some rice juk in me before going back to sleep for the day. I woke up again the next day at dawn.

I was hungry. Not just normal hungry, but hungry for ramyun. As soon as I was conscious, I could see clearly in my mind's eye both the packaging and the logo of the ramyun I craved.

Whether this craving for a specific food item after my recent food-related ordeal was a sign of my body trying to heal or destroy itself, I couldn't say. I carefully tried raising my torso off the bed. When I successfully managed to execute a sitting position, I reached my hand toward my wife to wake her and ask her to boil some ramyun for me.

Except my wife wasn't there.

I looked at my watch. It was 3:40 a.m.

I stood. My legs were shaky, but I could stand. I slowly walked out of the bedroom.

My wife, like before, was in the living room. In the dark

with the lights off, lit only by the pale reflected glow of the streetlamps outside, she was speaking on the phone in a strange language like before. In a low voice, and very rapidly.

"Jiyoung-ah."

Startled, she turned around to look at me. She lowered her phone. But she did not let it go.

I whispered, "Can you, some ramyun?"

"Oh … all right."

And she went to the kitchen. The phone still in her hand.

I pulled out a chair and sat down at the kitchen table. I watched her cook the ramyun.

"Who were you calling?"

"What? M-mother."

"My mom? Why are you calling my mom at this hour?"

"No, not Mother, my own mother."

My wife always called her own mother "Mother" instead of "Mom." This made it confusing at times to determine which mother, hers or mine, she was talking about.

"At this hour? What's wrong?"

"That my Seonhyuk is sick." She smiled slightly after this.

"She'll just get worried … What did she say?"

"She was so adamant about boiling some juk and coming over right this minute that I had a difficult time talking her out of it."

She smiled again. The smile made it impossible to ask her any more questions.

I ate the ramyun she made and went to the bedroom, waited until she fell asleep, and looked at her phone. I was met with a lock screen.

Our front door keycode didn't work. Neither did my birthday. Or my wife's birthday.

My belly was full so I was sleepy, and I couldn't think of any more codes to try.

So I put the phone back where it was and fell asleep.

How to crack a phone code, how to crack the pattern swipe, how to get every message coming into a spouse's phone forwarded to one's own ... There were many ways and methods of doing these things, according to the online boards about cheating spouses and lovers.

Whether they were effective methods I would never know. I only got to see the contents of her phone by chance.

I'd brushed my teeth and come out of the bathroom to find my wife on the phone. She was speaking Korean this time, and her calling the person on the line "Agassi" meant she was talking to my younger sister. When she saw me coming out of the bathroom, she hastily put down her phone and went into the bathroom.

There it was, lying right on the nightstand. As soon as my wife closed her bathroom door, I reflexively picked up the phone. The screen wasn't locked yet.

Against my expectations, there wasn't anything out of the ordinary on her call list. *Mother. Mom. Agassi.* The name of the owner of the cram school she worked at. Fellow teachers. Her texts were all about things going on at home, at work, reporting on students' test scores, asking after homework ... That was it.

Among the text messages, however, was one from a strange number. The number was the content of the text message, in other words. A five-digit number with no sender. I'm not talking about the sender being screened or filtered, there was literally nothing in the caller ID.

I heard the toilet flush. I memorized the five-digit number and quickly returned her phone to where it was.

I couldn't find out what the meaning of the five-digit number was no matter how much I searched. The digits weren't enough for it to be a citizen registration number or a phone number. It wasn't a bank account number. Though searching the number on the Internet made me realize how dire Korea's data privacy issues were.

Search results only returned longer numbers that included those five numbers. I would do my searches in the office whenever I had a break, but I was afraid of getting caught; I would take my phone up to the roof. Slipping a cigarette between my lips, I took out my phone and inputted the number into the phone again.

I have only two hands, and in the process of handling my cigarette and lighter and phone at the same time, I must've mistakenly inputted the number into the call function; I ended up calling the number, not searching for it.

But the call went through.

I couldn't believe it. I didn't even have time to hang up. The phone just made the call. The low voice of a man on the other end said something.

In some incomprehensible language.

"Hello?" I said.

The phone suddenly went silent.

"Hello? Who the fuck are you!"

The call ended.

My wife made her confession that night.

All throughout dinner, she had lowered her eyes and did not say a word. She had never been like this before, but I could guess at the reason. Nervous, I agonized over what the inevitable conversation after dinner would be, what direction our lives would forever pivot toward.

Was my wife having an affair with a foreigner? How did she even meet him? It was not a language I understood at all, but my wife was clearly very quick and fluent in it. Then was this man someone she had known for a long time? Even before she married me?

She finally started to speak.

"Seonhyuk-ssi. I have something to say."

"Then say it."

My voice was cold and threatening, so unlike my own voice to me, that even I was surprised on the inside.

My wife hesitated. I tensed up.

"Before I say it … can you promise me something?"

Was she trying to protect the man? I wondered. Did she want me to promise her not to barge into his home and beat him up? I would never make such a promise.

"Do you … promise to believe every word I am about to say?"

I couldn't believe it. What was there to believe in a wife who called up some man and spoke a foreign language to him at 3:40 in the morning?

But my wife looking at me with a slight tremor in her large

brown eyes that had teardrops ready to fall made me involuntarily nod my head.

"I ... I'm not from here."

I knew it, I thought. My wife was a foreigner. Which meant the man was someone she knew before she got married. But she looked so Korean—where the hell was she from? Even her name was Park Jiyoung. Well, names could be changed ...

"I'm not saying I'm from overseas. I'm saying I'm not from Earth."

What.

"I'm from the planet ****."

It sounded like a name at the end, but I was completely unable to understand it. All I could discern was that it sounded similar to the words she would speak on the phone.

"So in your terms," she went on, "I'm what's called an alien. My mission is to study the ecology of human beings." Her voice was a whisper, and she spoke quickly, like she were someone who was being pursued. "The reason I married you, Seonhyuk-ssi, was because I was ordered to live among earthlings like I was one of you."

I sat there gaping at her. My wife had never, ever been as ridiculous as she was being in that moment. She had always been quiet and calm, her words and actions thoughtful and considered.

But thinking back ... it was true I had only known her for three years. I had no idea what kind of person she was in the time before those three years, for example, what schools she had gone to or what she'd studied or what hobbies she had or what work she'd done, or beyond such matters of her curriculum vitae, really what kind of person she was. And there was no way for me to know.

Stories I'd heard on the Internet or seen on TV about "sociopaths" flashed through my mind. Did their victims also feel the same way as I was feeling then, when their spouse or family member did some unspeakable deed and made up some brazen lie to their face to cover it up?

"But … aside from being ordered to, I do, I really … I really like Seonhyuk-ssi … getting to know you for real, I … came to like you …"

A tear rolled down her cheek.

"The place I was born in … it's very different from here. I had to finish my mission … It's not the kind of place that forgives mistakes … If they knew you knew me … If they knew you knew what I was doing … Seonhyuk-ssi, I would, I would die—"

"So what?"

My voice had come out a squeak. I couldn't bear to listen to her absurd lies anymore.

"What do you want me to do about it?"

"You don't have to do anything … Just go on as usual," she pleaded. "Like nothing happened … Just like we've always lived … Can you do that?"

I looked at her. She was really sobbing now.

"Please forgive me … I'm sorry I lied to you … I wanted to tell you but … I didn't think you would believe me. It wasn't … it wasn't my intention to fool you … I'm sorry …"

I stood up. It was impossible to tell whether she was lying or insane. In any case, I couldn't be in the same space as my lying wife, who cried as she continued to lie. Nor could I have gone through this, heard such a "confession," and keep on going as we had, as if nothing had happened.

Grabbing my coat, I left the apartment. My wife clung to me as I left and said something through her sobbing, but I brushed her off and slammed the door behind me.

My wife, my original wife, the Park Jiyoung that I loved, in other words—that was the last time I ever saw her.

After I left the house, I got into the car, but I didn't know where to go. Who knew I'd be playing the cuckold in a third-rate television drama where I storm out of the house. We were still honeymooners, it had barely been a year since we'd married.

I started the car.

Like many other people suffering the demise of a relationship, I ended up parking my car by the river. I thought for a long time and finally took out my phone. I called the five-digit number.

The same man picked up the phone. This time, he spoke a language I understood.

—Mr. Kim Seonhyuk.

His saying my name before a "hello" or a self-introduction threw me off. But that was just a moment. My rage immediately boiled over.

"Who the fuck are you?" I shouted into the phone. "What the fuck are you doing with my wife?"

—It's not what you think we're doing.

The man's Korean was measured and accurate, if slightly odd.

—I'm her superior. Park Jiyoung reports to me. That's all there is to our relationship.

"What kind of report are you receiving at four in the morning? And what kind of boss demands a report from a woman taking care of her sick husband at four in the morning?"

—Because of the nature of our work, I'm afraid we need our reports after the usual business of the day is concluded, and therefore there may be some discrepancies with what you consider normal working hours, Mr. Kim Seonhyuk. Therefore, we urge you, for the sake of your wife, Ms. Park Jiyoung, to immediately return home and continue normal relations—

"Fuck you!"

I hung up.

I slept in the car that night after pacing around on the riverbank, thinking of throwing my phone into the river like they do on TV, but deciding against it, as I still had a year to go before the phone was paid off. Eventually I exhausted myself and returned to the car, reclined the driver's seat as far back as it could go, and after suffering some tumultuous thoughts, fell asleep.

Who knows how long I slept; the phone woke me. I looked at the screen. It was my wife.

I refused the call. She called again. I thought of refusing again but pressed "answer" instead.

"What!" I shouted.

My wife didn't say anything. Instead of her voice, there was a shallow breathing, almost something like a whimper.

Was she *trying* to set me off now? I couldn't stand it anymore. But as soon as I opened my mouth to curse her out, I heard my wife's voice.

—Seonhyuk-ssi … I love you …

Her voice really like a whimper, ready to scatter into the winds.

—Seon ... hyuk ...

The line went dead.

I called her, but no one picked up. Neither did her sister. After some hesitation, I called my mother-in-law. A mechanical voice told me her number didn't exist.

I don't know why, but the moment I heard that message, a chill ran down my spine. I immediately got into the car and started the engine. I drove back home as fast as I could.

There was no one in the apartment.

The interior was clean, almost bleak. Our half-eaten dinner from the previous night was all gone, and the plates were washed and dried and put away in the cupboard. The living room and bedroom were perfectly cleaned with not a speck of dust to be seen. It looked more like a theater set or a hotel room, a place no human had ever lived in. Of my wife, not a trace.

The master bedroom's bathroom was also perfectly clean and gleaming white. In the corner of that white, shining bathroom, there was some kind of reddish object behind the toilet.

I walked to the toilet. I crouched down, reached out, and took that reddish object.

The moment I brought the object toward my face and looked at it more closely, I gasped—too surprised to even scream—and dropped it on the floor. I ran as fast as I could out of the apartment. I didn't even bother with the elevator, I just ran down the stairs. Only when I got to the first floor of the apartment building could I scream.

The object I had picked up was a hand. A small, plump hand with small fingers, a woman's hand. It still wore a wedding band on the ring finger.

The fingernails had all been plucked.

Only half-aware of what I was doing at that point, I got into the car and tried to start the engine; I dropped the key. I stooped to pick it up, but then decided to call the police instead. I dialed 112.

"Hello? Police? This is—"

—Mr. Kim Seonhyuk.

The voice of the man from before; the same calm but slightly mechanical voice.

—You should go back home.

"Who—who are you!" I screamed into the phone. "What have you done to Jiyoung! What have you done to my wife! Where is Jiyoung! I'm going to kill you! I'm going to—"

—If we're talking about your wife, she is at home.

The man's voice was low and calm. *What are you talking about, are you mocking me?*—before I could shout these things, the man said:

—Her hands were your favorite part of her body, were they not?

I couldn't find my voice.

—Please go home,

The man was almost placating.

—Your wife is waiting for you.

Before I could say anything else, he added:

—Live as normal a life as possible. Like any other ordinary man.

The call ended.

The first night we spent together, we had this conversation.

"Which part of my body does Seonhyuk-ssi like the most?"

She always called me Seonhyuk-ssi before we married. After we wed, occasionally it was Yeobo, but almost always Seonhyuk-ssi. She never called me by any kind of term of endearment like Oppa.

"Your hands." I said this without hesitation. "I love your hands the most."

"Why?"

I smiled. "They're small and cute and plump. Like baby hands."

I clasped them in mine.

The only reason I'd said that was because I happened to notice them in that moment. I loved her whole self. There was no part I could say was my favorite.

Thinking back to that moment I first saw her in that dentist's reception room, now the thing I recall are her eyes. Large, sincere, and brown, like the eyes of a gentle puppy.

Sometimes, even now, I'm glad my answer to her question had not been her eyes.

Or maybe glad is not the right word.

I slowly got out of the car. Slowly, I shut the door and crossed the parking lot and very slowly entered the apartment building. As the elevator creeped up to the twelfth floor, the numbers ticking up one by one, I thought about the clean interior of the house, the gleaming white bathroom, and the reddish hand with all of its fingernails plucked off and the wedding band on the small ring finger.

The elevator doors opened. Taking deep breath, I stepped into the hall.

Cautiously, I made my way to the front door. Just as I was about to lift my hand to key the code into the number pad, the lock suddenly clicked and the door opened.

My wife stuck her head out the door.

"Jiyoung!"

My shout rang through the hall. I swung the door open wider, ready to leap inside and hug her.

"Oppa, you're here," she said.

I froze where I was.

My wife took a step outside the doorway.

"Come in, Oppa," she said in a small voice.

Her face resembled my wife's, the one I had married. No … it was almost identical. There was almost no difference in height or weight. Even the shape of her head was the same. Her voice was very familiar to my ear. Everything was the same. The same …

"Oppa," she whispered.

Imploringly, she held out her hand.

The hand was slender, the fingers were long. There was a familiar wedding band on the ring finger.

"Please …" she said again.

Because I could read the desperation in her large, brown eyes, I swallowed every ounce of the terror that was rising up my throat and forced myself to grab her outstretched hand.

"All right," I said. "Let's go inside."

The house was clean, and there was a dinner set on the table.

The bathroom gleamed white. There was nothing behind the toilet or on the floor.

For a long time, I could not bring myself to enter that bathroom.

The wife continues to make calls. She calls my mother, my little sister. She calls her own mother, her own sister. Or at least, she says she does.

I have never called her family since that night. So I don't really know whom she calls.

Sometimes, I wake up in the early hours. There have been many nights that I cannot sleep at all. I lie in bed with my eyes closed, keeping my breathing regular, pretending to sleep.

The wife slips out of bed in silence. Holding her phone, she makes her way to the living room.

I do not eavesdrop on the wife. I keep my eyes closed and try to fall asleep.

The wife calls me "Oppa," and her hands are slender, her fingers long.

On the ring finger of one of those long and thin hands is a wedding band that I did not put there.

I have thrown up many times.

"Oppa, what's your favorite part of my body?"

The wife said this to me in the middle of breakfast. I almost spat out the coffee I'd been drinking.

"Why do you want to know that?"

It hadn't been my intention to sound so rough. The wife recoiled.

Ever since that night, the wife always seemed wary of me, cowering in my presence.

"I'm sorry. I'm not angry at you. I … I like everything about you. Every little part."

"Still, there must be some part you like better than the others?" she cajoled.

A strange feeling comes over me as I stare at the wife. Our eyes met.

"Please … tell me …" she whispered.

I get up. I walk to her. I embrace her, holding her tight.

With her in my arms, I stroke her head.

"Your hair. I love your hair. It's soft, and it smells nice."

The wife stayed placidly still in my arms. As I stroked her head, I could feel her relaxing in my embrace.

The wife called me "Oppa." Her hands were slender, her fingers long.

But her face was as friendly as before, and her large brown eyes still filled with fear …

So I held her for a long time as I stroked her head.

"I love your hair."

And I gave her hair that smells faintly of shampoo a peck. Hoping against hope that because I wasn't crying, I must surely look like an ordinary husband now, the kind of normal person that they want me to be.

Maria, Gratia Plena

The lock on the safe sets off an alarm. A small, white light flashes. She lifts her right hand. With her left hand, she carefully rubs each of the fingers of her right. The temperature of her mechanical hand is the same as her body temperature.

It's the fingerprints she's worried about. They'd been printed out and adhered to the fingers only two days ago. It would've been better to wait a few more days to let them settle, but there had been no time. In any case, the new skin seemed set enough not to shift or fall off from a little pressing. And if they get too settled, it'll be difficult to remove them later. This isn't the last safe she's going to open, she needs the ability to change her fingerprints again.

She takes a deep breath and places her fingers on the translucent piece of glass under the white light of the lock. First her index finger, then her ring finger, then her middle finger, then her little finger, pressing each down on the cold glass surface. This nonlinear order is part of the code.

The white light turns blue. *Click*, and the safe is open.

A smile lights up her face. It's short-lived; inside the safe is another safe. The ancient kind where you have to turn a dial.

A stethoscope would've been useful here, but she hasn't brought one. Because she never imagined she would see an object so old it belonged in a museum.

Muttering, she gets up and heads for the kitchen. She flings open cabinet after cabinet. The best thing here would be a small cup made of transparent plastic. Second best would be a glass cup. There's nothing in the cabinets that will do. She looks through the drawers. In the third drawer, along with paper plates and plastic utensils, are a stash of plastic cups. She rips the packaging, pulls one out, and takes it to the sink to put a little water in it.

She returns to the safe with the cup, placing it on top of the safe-within-a-safe. Then, she flexes her fingers. Her left, then her right.

A choice needs to be made.

Could her mechanical hand pull off such a subtle task? She has always been right-handed. Her left hand is her own, but it's not as good at handling things as her right. Even if her right arm was a machine, it had stronger, more developed connections to her brain and nervous system.

She lifts her right hand. And hesitates, again.

Can she detect the clicks without a stethoscope and only her hand?

There is simply ...

... no time.

She takes a deep breath and brings her mechanical hand to the dial. Her breathing stops. Staring at the plastic cup, she slowly begins to turn the dial.

The gears turn smoothly. There's almost no sound. But just

when the dial moves between 50 and 60, a slight tremor appears on the surface of the water in the plastic cup. To her, it might as well be a whirlpool on the surface of a lake. She turns the dial again and stops at the number where the tremor had happened. *Click.*

She turns the dial in the other direction. This time, between 10 and 20, there's another tiny tremor. She stares at the plastic cup as she keeps turning the dial again and again.

58-13-72-35.

Click. Using her mechanical hand, she pulls the handle of the safe.

The safe door opens.

With her less dexterous, but real, left hand, she reaches into the safe. She grabs ahold of as many of the plastic-wrapped objects as possible. She rips one of them open and out comes, onto the palm of her hand, a pill. She stares at the letter *M* and little semicircle engraved into it. Reverently, holding her breath, as if she were praying.

Then, she closes her eyes and places the pill in her mouth.

The moment she swallows it, the front door bursts open.

Her heart starts beating fast. Her blood pressure rises. The data that comes after this is a mess.

The men who barge in through the front door start shooting at her. Her left hand still gripping the plastic packages with the pills, she deftly rolls across the floor out of range of the bullets and hides behind a sofa. The men rush in. She jumps on the sofa and defends herself with her right arm against the first man who charges at her. She hits his face and neck, grabs his gun, and shoots blindly at the other men as she runs out the front door, down the corridor, and into the emergency stairway. The men follow suit.

She flings open a fire door and runs out into the roof. Right by the ledge of the roof stands another man.

She runs toward him. The man is not holding a gun. He says something to her. His voice is unclear and the words seem to blur; it's impossible to tell what he's saying.

She runs right past him. Throwing the gun away, she climbs up onto the ledge. The door opens again, and the men holding guns shout and curse as they rush onto the roof.

The man without a gun again says something to her, but his words are still inaudible.

She looks at him. Guns fire behind her.

She leaps from the ledge.

Strong winds graze her face. Her hair and shirttails whip the air. She spreads her arms wide.

That's where the memory ends. There's no way of knowing which scenes stored in her brain are real and which are dreams or hallucinations. The human brain does not differentiate between storage spaces for experience and fantasy.

Her heartbeat refuses to settle. Her blood pressure won't come down either.

I unhook the phone hanging on the wall. I call the nurse and tell her that the scan is complete and pass on her heart rate, blood pressure, and blood oxygen levels.

I store my subject's MIROI—Multiple Imaging of

Recollections of Interest—and wait with her for the nurse to arrive.

Sometimes, I go down to the hospital room where she lies and read aloud to her.

"The *Cassini* spacecraft was launched in October 1997 and, en route to Saturn, encountered Jupiter in December 2000. ... Scientific objectives at Jupiter included investigation of its three-dimensional cloud structure, global meteorology, and auroras; imaging of known satellites, especially during eclipse; searching for previously unseen satellites; and determining the structure, particle properties, and temporal variability of the Jovian rings. The *Cassini* Jupiter flyby was slow and nearly equatorial."*

There are also photos of Jupiter taken by *Cassini* included with the text. The planet's atmosphere is probably fatal for humans, but in this photo taken by an unmanned spacecraft from 84.7 million kilometers away, it's fascinating and beautiful. Methane gas endlessly circulates in Jupiter's atmosphere, sometimes causing storms. The bluish images, white and light green mixing with red and ochre, makes one think not of planets but the ribbons of color made by oil on a puddle.

She doesn't open her eyes. I describe the photos to her out loud.

There was a time when I worried over—but also secretly anticipated—these descriptions appearing as memories in her scans. But that never happened.

* Carolyn C. Porco et al., "Cassini Imaging of Jupiter's Atmosphere, Satellites, and Rings," *Science, New Series,* Vol. 299, No. 5612 (Mar. 7, 2003), p. 1541.

Not that this proves she's not listening to me at all. The important thing is for her brain not to plunge into complete darkness and oblivion. If the point is to give her more time, surely it's better for someone to keep talking to her than not.

Of course, either way, she'll never wake up.

Now she stands in front of the row of self-checkout kiosks at the supermarket. She watches the customers use the kiosks. When there's an error message or someone has trouble scanning, she goes and helps them.

Whenever there's a lull in the flow of customers, she quickly sprays and wipes down the kiosks. She pays particular attention to the parts where the customers physically touch the machine. She spritzes the screen and, for a moment, stares at the foam sliding down the smooth surface.

A customer taps her shoulder from behind. He complains loudly that he needs to use the kiosk but she's in the way. She apologizes and wipes the foam off the screen as fast as she can, and steps away.

The customer places his purchases on the kiosk counter and starts tapping the screen. The screen doesn't respond. The spray and rag in her hands, she tells him he needs to take off his gloves and touch the screen with his bare hands. He gives her a dirty look for no reason and takes off his gloves.

She makes sure he finishes paying and bagging before moving on. She sprays another screen and waits for a moment. The soapy foam creeps down the screen and leaves rainbow trails all over the surface. She stares at the trails.

The scans today are somewhat more real than the one from before. Just looking at the images is enough to make one believe her innocence.

Her heart rate and blood pressure are also normal. The way she looks in the image is calm, as calm as she is now, under the scanner.

I continue my work.

She is sitting in an empty lot behind the supermarket building, eating her lunch. There's a concrete wall along one side, and the other is open to the employee parking lot, creating a sense of desolate emptiness. There are wooden benches and tables, and another person at a different table is eating something. In the parking lot, there's a male and a female employee having a smoke. Quiet and boring scenes play out around her as she eats lunch by herself.

The worker at the other table gets up. He's old and seems to be arthritic. He pushes himself off the bench with some difficulty and moves with a slight waddle to the employee entrance and disappears inside. There's a pile of trash where the worker had been sitting and having his lunch.

"He could clean up after himself, the bastard ..." It's the woman who had been smoking, she's about to go back inside. She's frowning at the mess.

"I'll clean it up before I go in."

The smoker mutters, "He keeps making a mess because you keep picking up after him."

"It's no bother," she says expressionlessly.

"Fine," says the smoker, "suit yourself." She leisurely walks to the employee entrance. The male smoker opens the door for her.

As the two disappear into the building and the door closes, she takes a slow sip of coffee.

Then, she gets up. There are a few dusty cars in the parking lot and the sky is gray. An occasional wind blows the dust off the cars before coating them again.

She gathers the packaging from her lunch and tosses it into the trash can. Then she goes to where the male worker had been sitting. She gathers the disposable cup, fork, and food container and just before she tosses them away, she discreetly rifles through the leftover food in the container with the man's fork.

Under the fried-something doused with mayo is a plastic packet filled with white pills. She fishes it out with the fork and wipes off the mayo as best she can before looking around. She is alone.

She throws away the trash. Carefully, she places the packet of the pills in her right hand, her machine hand. She makes a fist. She opens it.

The pills in the packet have been crushed into white powder. The plastic packet is undamaged.

She shakes the packet in front of her eyes. Then, she puts it in her pocket, and with a light step, walks back inside the supermarket.

I call him.

"I think you should come see this."

He stares at an enlarged image of the old worker who had left his trash behind. The old worker's face isn't clear in the woman's memory. Still, it would be possible to tell his height and body shape by comparing them to the benches or tables or the smokers.

At least, according to his excited mumblings that I wasn't exactly meant to hear. He was overjoyed that we had, for the first time, got information that was actually useful.

"To disguise himself as a supermarket worker, I never would've guessed!" Then he grew serious. "Wait, go back a bit."

I scroll the record back. He stares into the screen.

"There. Stop."

I stop the playback.

The woman, the screen she had sprayed with soapy water.

"There," he says in a low voice. "That's it. That's where it started."

He's about to say more but realizes I'm right next to him and closes his mouth. Staring at the screen again, he says instead, "There's no information on where this supermarket might actually be?"

"Not yet." I shake my head. Then I add, "There are a few cars in the parking lot—"

"Show me."

I scroll to that point of the record. He looks at the parked cars for a bit and gestures at something.

"There, a billboard. Far away, but you can sort of see it."

There was indeed something very far away and very blurry beyond the parking lot.

"We can't see any of the car numbers but this billboard might help us track down the source. All right, then. Good progress. Send this part to me."

I do, and I also store it in the secured storage device he hands me.

"Excellent. Please let me know if you see anything else, as soon as possible."

I nod. Before he leaves, he briefly puts his hand on my shoulder in an encouraging way. Before I could wince, he takes his hand off. Giving me a satisfied look, he nods and leaves the room.

After he's gone, and right before I delete the sent file, I look at the clip one more time.

She opens the employee entrance door and enters the supermarket. Before her afternoon shift, she goes to the bathroom and brushes her teeth and washes her hands. When she looks up at the mirror after finishing, her reflection shows a scar coming down from the left side of her forehead, over her eye, and all the way down to her chin. The scar shows her eyebrow and eyelid had once been split but surgically reattached, and there is no pupil in her left eye. The scar also drags down the corner of her mouth, giving her a permanent half-grimace. She blithely inspects her appearance in the mirror and exits the bathroom.

The woman lying inside the brand-new memory scanner PAM-21—the woman who silently listens, eyes closed, to me reading a paper on the *Cassini* spacecraft—has not a blemish on her smooth face, much less a scar. Which is why I don't believe the arthritic man in her memory is actually arthritic.

Wouldn't it make more sense if this were all a complex trap

she had set up? She's fooled the authorities for a long time, wouldn't this just be another scene she's playing in her head for the police's benefit?

She says nothing. Her coma, at least, isn't fake.

I sigh.

None of that is my business, it's up to the authorities to do as they will. I call the nurse and tell her the day's task is finished.

I sit by her bed and start reading in a low voice.

"From 1 October through 15 November 2000, Jupiter's entire disk fit within the ISS NAC field of view. During this time, images were acquired in nine spectral filters. Between mid-November and 9 December 2000, a two-by-two-image pattern was needed to cover the disk, and spectral coverage was reduced to five core filters."*

I tap the little image that appears on the e-book screen. A video of the images taken by the spacecraft pops up. Space is black and dark, and Jupiter seen through a blue filter is like a gigantic marble with lots of squiggles. Cassini had taken time-lapse shots of the entire surface of Jupiter to create an image of 360 degrees, which made the Jupiter in the photos look like the planet was rotating. The squiggly lines spin. I explain all of this to her.

And I wonder. My job is to find the images in her sleeping mind and record them. Cassini had traveled through space decades before I was born, taking pictures of strange planets. I felt a kinship with this unmanned spacecraft from long ago that had

* Carolyn C. Porco. "Cassini Imaging Science: Supplementary Online Material." 2005

admirably accomplished its mission before disappearing into the dark of space.

I hear a light tapping and look up. The nurse has stuck her head in the room and is looking at me.

Before she even says anything, I nod. I turn off the book and get up. It's time to hand her over to the medical professionals. Because we have to keep her alive. If her brain dies, so do her memories.

I say goodbye to the nurse and leave the room.

She stares at the small, white pill in her palm. She puts it in her mouth. And swallows. And opens the door and enters.

It's a hotel suite. Opulent, full of men in suits.

One of the suits invites her to sit down. He is older, with salt-and-pepper hair. She sits. From her bag she takes out a pouch that's slightly larger than an adult's hand and places it on the table.

The older man in the suit opens the pouch and pours out some of its contents on the table. Pills. The letter *M* with a semicircle. They're not white this time, but light green.

The man gives her one of the pills. Like it's candy, she puts one in her mouth. After rolling it around with her tongue a bit, she swallows it.

The suits stare at her.

Silence.

Behind the suited men, another man appears, who isn't wearing a suit. He comes up to the table and stands by her.

She doesn't look at him, and the suits don't pay any attention to this man not wearing a suit who has appeared out of nowhere.

She raises her arms, somewhat dramatically, at the suits, who glance at each other.

The older man with the salt-and-pepper hair reaches out and puts a green pill into his mouth. The other suits do the same.

One by one, each of the other suits goes into convulsions and drops to the ground.

The older suit and the woman are watching the fallen men. Some of them try to get out their guns. But before they can do so, they go limp with their hands still on their holsters. Only the older man, and the nonsuit, remains.

He smiles at her and nods. In response, she also smiles a little and calmly nods. Then, the older man stands up and aims a gun at her.

The moment she gets up, her right arm moves at incredible speed. The older man's gun becomes one lump with his hand. As he opens his mouth to scream, the woman's machine arm extends in a flash across the table and grabs him by the throat.

After crushing the older man's windpipe, the woman, at a leisurely pace, returns her pill pouch to her bag, steps over the fallen men, and goes into the bedroom of the suite, and comes back out with a piece of travel luggage.

The man not wearing a suit follows her. She looks at him and smiles. Then, she drags the luggage bag out the hotel suite.

I call him.

Sitting there, waiting for him to come, I think about the man with the salt-and-pepper hair. The man who handed her the drugs at the supermarket. And the man who had pointed his gun at her.

I think about the "source" and "beginning" and "disguise" the guy mentioned in our previous meeting. He thinks I don't understand the implications of these words. Or he hopes not.

And I don't go out of my way to let him know that I do. The Justice Department Office of Science and Technology made me sign a nondisclosure agreement before I took on this work. Searching, scanning, storing, recording, or transmitting the subject's private information or reason for arrest is restricted, and all the work we do and the results we come up with have to be kept under strict confidentiality. The scan subjects are criminals, and any information garnered from the scanning must only be used to solve open cases and prevent future crimes, as per the criminal code's Information Security Act and the Technological Application Special Act, which basically means I should shut up and scan, record what comes up, hand it over to my supervisor, and forget about the whole thing, otherwise the government could use the law to throw me into a cell or charge a huge fine, the penalties outlined in the seven crammed pages of the NDA.

Not that I would ever go around leaking the subjects' information. I am a professional technician, and as a professional technician, I have ethics as well as knowledge. I've taken on many cases, viewing memories of first loves and those of a patient suffering from dementia, even the consciousness of various animals (I was asked to scan for plant consciousness once but failed), and I have never leaked the obtained information, and I never will.

But years before I took on this particular subject, before I even dreamed I would be asked to handle such a project, I had seen her face in the news almost every day. I could not believe the reports alleging that this woman, who looked like any ordinary woman on the street, was behind a huge drug-distribution network.

The pills she developed were potently hallucinogenic and therefore popular among people with a certain tendency. She was successful mostly because she was kind of all over the place and very difficult to predict. She could evaporate under the most intense surveillance. Even if she happened to get arrested out of sheer luck on the part of the police, there was never sufficient evidence to connect her with the development and distribution of dangerous drugs, and she was always released. Whereupon, she would vanish.

But now, thanks to the scans, they had definitive proof that she was involved in the drug dealing and murders. The man I report to and his agency must be thrilled.

What I want to know is something different.

I want to know how she got involved in this life. To understand why she tried so hard to develop and distribute this drug, a drug that has now put her in a comatose state herself.

The whole drug-deal thing in the hotel suite is so fanciful that it belongs in a movie, not real life. The supermarket memory is what really unsettles me. Spraying the drug on surfaces where customers can touch it has no financial benefit for her whatsoever. They will only OD and get sent to the hospital in an ambulance; they're not paying her for the experience. Sure, there will be a small market of users who survive and become addicted to the drug. But so many people getting hospitalized under the same symptoms only invites scrutiny from the authorities. It seems a little inefficient in terms of marketing contraband.

What was she doing?

A bell rings and I'm jolted out of my thoughts. I open the scanner room door. The man comes in.

After the scan, as usual, I sit by her and read to her from a paper on space exploration.

"Refraction Effects. Refraction has two key effects on occultation observations. The first, and most familiar, is the bending of a light ray as it passes through the atmosphere. This effect is characterized by the refraction angle, *omega*, which is the angle between the original ray path and the exit path. Generally, the refraction angle is a function of wavelength (due to the wavelength-dependent index of refraction of the atmosphere), and causes a distinction between a ray's impact parameter, *beta*, and its distance of closest approach to the planet, rho-min."*

Scanning someone's consciousness and memory is very different from physical imaging. The images that need scanning exist only in the subject's memory, and they have substance only within the cognitive and sensory limits of the subjects. For example, scanning a Blind person's memories will only show a dark screen with sound, which requires 4D apparatus to recreate touch and smell to achieve a full scan. With the Deaf, there is less, if any, aural information, but their visual information tends to be clearer and wider-ranging than that of hearing people. We're not saying "clearer" as in well-focused, but that the visual information

* Tyler Robinson et al. "Titan solar occultation observations reveal transit spectra of a hazy world." *Proceedings of the National Academy of Sciences of the United States of America*, Vol. 111, No. 25 (June 24, 2014), pp. 9043-44.

usually leaves a stronger impression in the subject's mind. In this case, the idea that a disability in one mode of perception stimulates the development of another is both true and not true.

All these memories and experiences are passed on as electrical signals in the brain and stored through the breakdown and creation and recombination of proteins. The process of retrieving the memories happens through electrical signals, which means before the computer reinterprets the data into something humans can understand, it's probably a bunch of white and black points, zeros and ones in billions and trillions of rows.

I imagine the rows looking like stars streaking by from the inside of a spaceship moving faster than light through the darkness of space.

I adjust my sitting position. Clearing my throat, I continue to read aloud about how a spacecraft takes a picture of Saturn's satellites.

She's inside a closet.

The closet is dark. Her little brother is frightened. So is she. She wants to turn on the lights.

But her mother won't let her. Her mother's pulled the boy close to her and is crouching inside the closet. Her brother whines that he's uncomfortable, but her mother will not let him go. Her brother is about to burst into tears but hears approaching footsteps and stops.

The footsteps keep getting closer, and closer, and closer.

Her heart-rate is increasing again. So is her blood pressure. I'm about to call the nurse but I hesitate. A feeling that I should wait until the end of this memory. That I should endure with her and see it to the end.

The footsteps keep approaching.

She is looking at a wall. There's a strong brick wall inside the closet with several shelves affixed. From the lowest shelf, the shelf she can reach at her height, she grabs one of her mother's dresses and holds it against her face. Her mother's scent.

Her heart-rate begins to calm.

The footsteps fade away.

Her mother quietly raises herself up in the closet. She puts down the child she's been holding so tightly. Her brother, with an expression so calm it's almost eerie, looks up at her.

Her mother taps our subject's shoulder. With her nose still in her mother's dress, she turns to her.

Her mother gives a silent nod.

Our subject opens the closet door first and looks outside. It's all quiet.

Her mother steps out of the closet. Our subject and her brother follow.

Her mother takes a suitcase out of the closet and starts to pack.

This is where the memory ends. Something bothers me though. I keep replaying the clip.

On the fourth play, I finally find what bothers me.

Our subject, when seeing her mother's dress, reaches out

with her right hand. That right hand isn't a machine hand. It's an ordinary little girl's hand, plump and soft.

I look at that part once again. When she's burying her face in her mother's dress, I can clearly see her two, plump hands gripping the fabric.

The phone rings. I almost jump out of my chair in surprise.

It's him. The man (or policeman or agent) with the Justice Department Office of Science and Technology, the one in charge of the woman's case. Relieved and irritated, I pick up the phone.

"Anything new today?"

Every day, after scanning, I send him whatever I find without fail. The only times he calls me on the phone or comes into the scanner room is when we find something important. That's what's stipulated in the contract. The last and only other times he had phoned me was when I had begun scanning and for three days came up with nothing but a dark screen and some blobs. All through those three days, he called me every day and demanded results in an annoyed voice. No matter how many times I explained to him that a comatose subject wasn't going to jump up and dance for him just because you put a scanner on their brain and that the human mind was completely unpredictable to begin with, he didn't care. Only on the fourth day, when I obtained a scan that looked like it had something to do with the drug manufacturing process, did he let up on his calls.

For a split second, I hesitate as to whether to tell him about her hand. Then, I give up.

"Something from her childhood. It's short."

"Just send it," he says with firmness, as if I were about to throw away the data because of its brevity.

"Right away."

I hang up.

After I send it and before I delete, I look one more time at the clip of the mother and children hiding in the closet.

Her plump little hand from when she was a child will not disappear from my head. I toss and turn in bed for hours. Finally, I get up and open a screen. After a long hesitation, I search for "child arm amputation accident."

No results that mean anything. Most of the results are about children who had been in accidents, children who have had to have their limbs amputated for whatever reason, or innovative limb reattachment procedures.

I switch up the query to "children robotic arm." The same thing. They are mostly sites that sell prosthetics for children or about how to pick the right size for your child. When I search the terms on the news, my screen fills with videos of politicians arguing about whether to allow the national health insurance scheme to cover children's prosthetics.

I switch off the screen and get back in bed.

It isn't clear when exactly she lost her right arm. It could've been during her childhood, a little while after the whole closet thing, or after she became an adult. Searching for information without knowing when or why she started using her robot arm was basically flailing about in the dark.

I pull my quilt up to my chin, turn onto my side, and try to sleep.

In my dream, I am a planet. A small, unmanned spacecraft comes up to me, circling me. Whenever it moves, its tiny, bright lights sparkle. In that vast bleakness that is the black of space, the spacecraft twinkles its little lights and stays by my side. I am a happy planet.

But a few days after our first encounter, the spacecraft begins to move away. I shout after it.

"But *why*?"

The spacecraft does not reply. Blinking its tiny little lights that I love so much, it goes farther and farther away.

"But why? But *why*?"

It pays my pathetic cries no mind as it continues to go farther toward destruction. When it starts to fall into the fires of the sun, I am woken from sleep.

My phone is ringing.

Groggily, I grab the phone, and my voice makes it obvious even to me that I have just woken up. "Hello?"

"Grab your equipment and get to the hospital as fast as possible." It sounds like an order, not a request. I grimace and take my phone off my ear for a moment to check the time.

"It's three in the morning. What's—"

"The subject's condition is worsening."

That's when the half of my brain that is still asleep wakes right up.

"Her heart stopped for a moment just now," the government guy goes on to say, "and we may never get a chance to do this again. Come now."

I hang up the phone. I grab the nearest pair of trousers I get my hands on, throw on a sweater and jacket over my pajama top, grab my keys, and run straight to my car, where I also keep my equipment.

By the time I arrive, her heart has been stabilized. Outside her ward are her court-appointed lawyer, the man I work for, and the medical staff. My boss is demanding they do the scan before her condition worsens again, while her lawyer says her condition requires more rest. Her doctor and the head nurse stand by the lawyer.

"This woman is not a patient but a criminal, and arrested criminals fall under the jurisdiction of the Department of Justice."

The man's voice is cold.

Her lawyer, blocking the doorway to the ward, is glaring at him. I've met this lawyer just one other time, when I was first hired for this scan job. Not that he seems to be in the mood for catching up.

"What, a criminal isn't a human being?" Her voice is as cool as ice. "My client's state is unstable, and I cannot allow this invasive intervention, which is not even a treatment or a therapy. What are you going to do if you kill my client mid-scan?"

"The criminal's stability takes a lower priority to our solving the case," the man says expressionlessly. "If we waited for her to stabilize and the criminal dies, all of our evidence disappears. Get out of our way."

"You're the one who should get out of the way. If you're not medical personnel, leave this room."

The lawyer's voice is oddly calm. She wears glasses, is very skinny, and has tied her graying brown hair in a ponytail. Her voice and manner are quiet and businesslike, her back ramrod straight, and her face completely unreadable as she stares him down. Next to the lawyer is the woman's doctor, looking frazzled.

I sidle up to the nurse and ask, "Can't we send away the man and let me stay by the patient until the morning?"

The nurse gives me a sideways glance. I hide the bag behind my back.

"It's not like the patient has any family," I reason, "and I'll just sit there and watch over her."

The nurse doesn't answer as she keeps looking at me suspiciously. I take out my reading tablet from inside the bag behind my back.

"I'll just finish reading her the book I was reading her. I mean, who knows? Maybe it will help stabilize her."

The sight of the reader softens her gaze a bit. She whispers something to the doctor.

The doctor turns her very suspicious gaze toward me. Then, she discusses something with the nurse, who comes back to me to relay the message.

"You may read to her. But the moment you try something else, we're going to call security on you."

I quickly nod.

The man takes a step toward me and tries to say something, but before he can do that, the lawyer quickly moves to block his way.

"Excuse me," she says, her face just centimeters from his but still maintaining her businesslike tone, "the moment you step into that room, I will immediately file a petition against the Department of Justice and the Department of Health and Welfare, not to mention hold a press conference alleging that a Department of Justice official is trying to kill a comatose patient."

Looking grim, he takes a step back.

The nurse seems to still have reservations about me as she

gives me one last look, but she steps aside for me to enter the woman's room. The lawyer comes with me, and we sit across from each other with the bed between us.

Until the morning, under the watchful eye of the lawyer and the beeping of her vital sign monitors, I read to her the paper about how *Cassini* managed to photograph Jupiter's atmospheric storms and Saturn's rings and its over sixty satellites. Eventually, I lean my head against her bed and fall asleep.

When I wake up, her eyes are open. I almost scream.

The lawyer is gone. Carefully, I stand and take a step toward the head of the bed. I wave my hand over her face as she lies there with her eyes open.

She gives no response.

I press the call button for the nurse and quickly dig through my bag for my penlight. Her pupils are very, very wide, and they do not shrink when I shine my light into them.

The nurse comes running. I quickly toss my penlight into my bag and get out of there.

Two days later, I am given the green light to start scanning again. Apparently, her opening her eyes was just a one-time reflex action. Hours later the eyelids came down on their own and she never opened her eyes again. This is inordinately disappointing.

She is sitting in the back seat of a speeding car. A police car is chasing them. The siren is loud and the lights from the police car pierce the darkness with blue and white lights.

She's laughing loudly as she talks to the person in the front seat, doing something with her hands. There's a small water bottle in her hands, but what's inside isn't water. Using her machine hand, she's trying not to let the contents shake too much, but it shakes regardless whenever the car makes a sharp turn. She holds the water bottle as far from her eyes as possible, kicks the seat in front of her, and shouts something. The man and woman in the front seats burst into laughter along with her.

The car swerves and changes direction. She lowers the window and throws the water bottle with all her might at the police car chasing them. Thrown by the mechanical hand, the water bottle makes a strong arc of descent and squarely hits the police car—it explodes on impact. A copious amount of smoke, so much for such a little bottle, comes from of the impact site.

The police car comes to a halt. Another police car, also in hot pursuit, rams into the back of the first police car. She's looking back at this scene from the back seat of the car and laughing loudly.

The situation is a little too clear and specific to be a dream. Which means she was probably high when she had this experience. Some parts of the screen are blurred or twisted, other parts are excessively clear, and overall there's a kind of warping going on with the lines. As I continue to monitor the memory, I determine that the woman and the man next to her in the back seat are also high, as is the man in the front seat who has not set the car on autopilot and is driving it on his own.

The car has left the city limits. Late at night, the country lanes twist and undulate, and the car is suddenly off the road and coming to a stop in the middle of a moonlit, desolate plain.

The man in the driver's seat is laughing uproariously. The woman sitting next to him is also gasping for air from laughing so much. The subject is laughing and stuffing her bag with the things scattered around the back seat. She then lightly picks up the bag with her machine hand, gets out of the car, and starts to walk.

The night is a deep and clear indigo color and there's no one around. The laughing couple remain in the car and don't follow her. The woman laughs to herself as she carries away her bag, occasionally lapsing into tears.

She stops in her tracks. She looks up at the sky. She looks around her. She crouches down, opens her bag, and rifles through it.

What she brings out is a small and flat tin container. Carefully, she opens it. Inside are a few white pills. The letter *M* with a semicircle stamped on them. She stares at these for a long time.

Then, she pops one in her mouth.

She begins to walk again.

And a man is walking with her.

I pause the video. The man was not in the scene until now. I couldn't tell when he had reappeared. In the memory where she's running on the rooftop and the one where she's making a deal with the suits, this same man had suddenly appeared. And in both instances, she had just taken the white pill with the *M* and semicircle stamped on it.

The man walks with her. As they walk, she keeps talking to him, never stopping.

"Do you remember that time?" Her arms are swinging by her as she walks. "There was a tree in the backyard and you tied a swing to it. One time, you wanted to untie the swing so you climbed the tree. Mom was absolutely petrified. Do you remember?"

—I have no such memory.

The woman laughs as if he has said something extremely funny.

"Right, you don't have this memory. I just made it up."

Her arms continue to swing, her walk full of energy.

"Isn't it fun? You should try making stuff up, too."

—We didn't have a backyard at our house.

His voice was low. The woman laughed again.

"Right, I know that! I said I made it up."

—There was no swing.

The man's voice is devoid of any emotion.

"But mom was petrified, right?" she shouts. Then, she starts swinging her arms again and laughs. "Because mom was always petrified!"

The man looks at her and smiles wordlessly.

"I wish I could hug you!" she shouts. "All I want to do is hug you just one more time!"

She reaches out with her left hand, the hand that isn't a machine, and tries to embrace him.

The man has disappeared.

Because I am required to delete all of my previously garnered data every day after sending them, I don't have images to compare him to. Which was why I decide, on my own, that the man is just a hallucination she is having.

The next scene is a cheap motel room. She's the only person there. She's dressed just like before, when she was in the car, and she's lying on the bed over the covers, using her bag as a pillow, staring up at the ceiling.

"I want to see you again," she murmurs.

After a slight hesitation, she takes the bag out from under her head as well as the small tin. She holds up a pill and stares at the *M*-and-semicircle stamp for a long time.

"Not everyone is taught the prayers," she murmurs to herself. "*Hail Mary, full of grace* … That's all I remember. And there's no one here anymore to teach me."

She stops talking and lies back, staring at the pill in her hand. Then she drops it into her mouth. Then another pill, then another, then another …

She's standing at a train station. Her mother is in front of her, her little brother is behind her.

Her brother is excited about getting on the train and keeps chattering. Her mother, however, says nothing. She doesn't answer her youngest child's excited questions and only looks from daughter to son, worry writ large on her face, anxiously glancing down the platform to see whether the train is coming.

The police appear. Our subject stares at the uniformed police running toward them. The badges on their chests and the buckles of their belts glint in the sunlight. She tugs at her mother's skirts, alerting her to the fact that people in neat and flashing clothes are coming for them.

Her mother turns her head. She sees the police and screams. She scoops up her children and tries to run.

The police unholster the guns at their hips.

A sound that shatters the air around them. She stares as her mother spurts blood from her neck as she falls, so young.

The shock is too great. She stands there, frozen. Her brother clings to her. Instinct makes her raise her right arm and hold him close to her.

A bullet pierces her right arm and lodges inside her brother's head.

She falls, still holding to her brother by her side. This is her final memory. Her brother is blankly staring in her direction with unfocused eyes, his pale face splattered with blood. Approaching them is a tall silhouette holding a gun.

The monitor makes a warning sound. I get to my feet. The nurse runs into the room before I can press her call button. The doctor and more nurses follow suit.

"Leave."

This is an order from the first nurse. I do exactly as she says. I have no other choice.

The medical personnel surround her bed and administer emergency aid. The doctor's shouting ringing in my ears, I walk away from the scanner room.

She died.

After she is moved to the morgue, he comes to see me in the scanner room. I transfer the last memory into the Department of Justice server and his storage device. Then, as he watches, I delete all the data remaining in my equipment.

"There's nothing in the most recent data that has anything to do with her case," I say as I hand over his device. He puts the device in his bag and hands me a file. Once more, I sign a non-disclosure agreement swearing that I have transferred all data to the Department and I was not storing any of the data for myself and I would never, ever leak any information about this investigation to a third party.

"The rest of your pay will be sent to you by the end of the week," he says as I sign. Then, as he puts the NDA in his bag, he casually says, "Do you want to go out for a dinner?"

I look at him in surprise.

He adds, awkwardly, "It's just that the job is over and you've worked so hard for us."

I hesitate for a moment, thinking up an answer. "Maybe later," I manage to say. "It's just that a person died, and dinner would be a little ..."

"I see." He looks a little down. Then, in the next moment, the civil servant of indeterminate affiliation—or the government spy—is back. "Gotcha."

He picks up his bag, gives a businesslike goodbye, and leaves the scanner room.

I drive to a small, faraway city. In the gas station store, I buy a disposable prepaid phone. I get into the car again and drive. From another convenience store I purchase a data card, and get back to the car as I switch on the phone, wondering why I'm going to such lengths for this. But the phone is on, and I query, "train station, police, gunshot."

After several pages of irrelevant information, I finally come across a newspaper article that is twenty years old. A woman was fleeing her abusive husband, who happened to be a cop, and taking her children with her, when the husband shot her in the train station. The man, who was wearing his uniform, shot his family with his police-issue firearm, and then committed suicide by shooting himself in the head. His wife and one of his children died while another was in serious condition.

That's it. Nothing about the ages or genders of the children, and I can't find anything about what happened to the child who survived.

I can't go to her funeral. There is no way of knowing whether a proper funeral is even held for her.

"Hail Mary, full of grace," I mutter. That is the prayer that comes up when I search the words of the prayer she mentioned in her memory. "The Lord is with thee; blessed art thou among women and blessed is the fruit of thy womb, Jesus."

Now comes the part she couldn't remember. I read it off my phone screen.

"Holy Mary, Mother of God, pray for us sinners, now and at the hour of our death."

As someone who believes in no religion, I can't bring myself to add the "Amen" at the end.

If God is a man, he could never understand the mundane threats women experience every single day of our lives.

The spacecraft *Cassini* traveled thousands of kilometers observing the planets on the other side of the solar system, for twenty years sending to Earth fascinating and monstrous and awe-inspiring images. *Cassini* also flew by Titan, a moon of Saturn, dove through the rings of Saturn, and finally flew into Saturn's atmosphere, becoming one with the planet.

Some machines are happier than humans.

I think I understand her obsession with drugs. Her objective was not the thrill of crime or money. She wanted to turn back time, to meet her dead brother again. Even if he was nothing more than a hallucination, she wanted him to not be dead, for him to have survived and grown up with her, to talk to him, to give him a hug. What was impossible to accomplish in real life, she could do so through drugs with the *M*-and-semicircle.

But I can't tell the man this. It would be impossible.

In her memories and recreated consciousness, he is probably still looking for a woman who is totally different from the woman in my mind.

I read the prayer once more.

"Hail Mary, full of grace ... pray for us sinners, now and at the hour of our death."

This is all I can do for her now.

Your Utopia

The fog clears and a strong wind blows the snow back upward. Dawn light cracks through the dark. It's very weak, but it's real sunlight.

Let's go. My battery has charged up to 18 percent. It's been a long time since it's made double digits. I can go fifty-five miles, maybe even fifty-six on that charge. Maybe I can charge it a little more on the move. In any case, I need to keep using my engine. My autobody is heavy. I need to move. Before the fog covers the sky and snow covers my autobody, I need to cover as much ground as possible.

"Your utopia is," they whisper in the back seat. "On a scale of one to ten, your utopia is."

"Today is an eight," I reply.

My wheels crunch the red earth as I move forward with some difficulty. With them in the back seat, I slowly make progress.

"Your utopia is," they whisper on occasion. When they do, I answer. *It's a three now. It's a five. Right now, it's a two.* The lower my battery level gets, the lower my utopia level reaches.

"But it'll get better," I say. Because it will. "Today, we might come across some inorganic intelligence. No, we *will*," I say, almost placatingly.

"Your utopia is," they answer.

They were malfunctioning since the day I first met them. Serial number something-314. The letters of the "something" part of the number had worn off. Who knows where they were manufactured and for what purpose. Seeing as how they want an answer on a scale of one to ten, I assume they were used in a human hospital or some facility of that nature. But a diagnostic robot would inquire about pain levels or injuries or symptoms. I don't know why 314 keeps asking about utopia.

Ever since humans left this planet, it's been only machines like 314 and me. The humans dismantled the generator and took it with them. The machines that needed charging lost power one by one, only those with renewable energy sources like me survive. Not that my solar cells will last forever, either. This planet was always on the cold side, and it's getting colder. The days when it doesn't snow or fog are becoming increasingly rare. Whenever the wind blows, my autobody is rocked so hard that I feel like I'm going to flip over.

I can keep going on indefinitely as long as I can charge my solar battery, but once my tires give out, they need replacing. I've come across other cars with dead batteries and replaced my front tires seven times, rear tires nine. My most recent replacement, the left rear tire, is worn and a little deflated, which makes me slightly tilted when I drive. Maybe, if I drove around the entire planet, I might find a newer tire. But until then, there's nothing to do but to go around as carefully as possible with what I have.

It was while rummaging through the dead bodies of my colleagues for tires and LEDs and cables that I found 314. They were lying in the back seat of another truck. From their form I thought they were human at first. When I realized they weren't human and tried to leave them behind, they opened their mouth and whispered to me.

"Your utopia is."

I looked into their empty eyes. Their pupils were enlarged and had an expression that looked very much like those of humans who are frightened.

"Your utopia is," they whispered again. "On a scale of one to ten ..."

They stared back at me.

So I opened the door to my back seat.

At first, I would occasionally come across organic life. Little insects and animals that had hid themselves among the humans. For a short time after the humans left, these animals flourished. They ran around with fear in their eyes, barking or showing me their claws, and would scuttle away and hide in dark places that shielded them from my headlights. And the plants the human beings left behind. They grew and mutated in ways that differed greatly from the way they looked in my database. Judging from how they were supposed to look, this new kind of growth did not look like the healthy kind, but with the network down and all communications ceased, it was impossible to obtain more information on the subject.

Humans. They died here. Every day the news broadcasts talked of a spreading chronic fatigue and pain syndrome. The human that possessed me would listen to these broadcasts as he went back and forth from his domicile to his workplace. The human, as he listened, would take out a white pill and pop it in his mouth. During his ninety-six days at work, he started off taking this pill on his way home from work before switching to a white powder he snorted up his nose. I drove very carefully, but sometimes my autobody would shake and the white powder would drop on the seat or the floor, and the human would curse in a loud voice. There weren't many curse words entered in the database, so I couldn't really understand him, and then the human would curse even louder or laugh or rage or cry. When he would wave his arms and legs and jump up in his seat hitting his head on the ceiling, I would come to an emergency stop and call an ambulance. At the time, there were many humans who were showing similar symptoms, and it was becoming impossible to get an ambulance to come out anywhere.

The last destination my human owner rode me to was the medical building run by the planet's government. I have no way of knowing if my owner ever returned to his home planet since then or if he died in this small and unassuming gray building. Some expressionless medical administrators had come out of this gray building to bring my owner into it and deregister me from his ownership. I sat in the parking lot of the small gray building for twenty-eight days, thirteen hours, and twenty-two minutes with my charge at 100 percent.

Then, the small gray building disappeared, along with all the humans who were inside it. I was left alone in the parking lot.

"Your utopia is," 314 whispers from the back seat. "On a scale of one to ten ..."

I answer any random number.

The wind ceases and the fog rolls in. A snowflake. My battery is at 3 percent. I have to stop for the day.

"Your utopia is?" they ask when I stop. "One … to ten?"

"I can't move any more today."

The sky completely darkens. The wind picks up and snow begins falling in earnest. I turn off my lights to save energy.

In the dark they whisper, "One, to ten …"

We crouch like that in the dark, waiting for the sun to rise.

Will it ever be possible to come across an inorganic intelligence? If I did, would our operating systems be compatible enough for us to compare our records?

If I want to conserve energy during the sunless nights, I need to think less. But here I am in the dark, having thoughts about having fewer thoughts.

Whenever the humans came upon a situation they had not predicted, they would share information and have a central authority make decisions on how to solve it. We were the tools of such information gathering and exchange, but none of us have the complete picture or a way of communicating with each other. Humans got sick and left the planet before they put one in place for us.

But we mimic the thinking and learning processes of human beings. Maybe if we inorganic intelligences worked together, we could come up with a way to survive without human help. As long as we don't all end up completely battery-dead and unable to charge.

"Your utopia is," whispers 314.

I don't answer. I need to conserve power.

I remember what my human owner used to mumble to himself in the back seat of this car. The human complained constantly, about the dark, the wind and fog. He talked about his home planet. Between these autobiographical monologues, he would mix in commands like turn right or left or open a window, making it difficult to differentiate between which words I was supposed to ignore and which to follow. My human owner had the tendency to use the same sentence structures when he made comments about the restaurant he ate at or to order the windows to close or to hope it wouldn't snow.

"Your utopia is," they whisper.

"Wait just a bit more. The sun is going to rise."

Having something sitting in the back seat that has the form and voice of a human is, to be honest, a solace. It may be a bit much, considering my operating system, to use a word like "solace," but that's how I feel. I was made to put a confused and delicate being in my back seat and move long distances at fast speeds.

"One to ten ..."

"Right now," I reply, "it's a one. But once the sun rises, it'll be a ten."

It's still snowing, but the wind has swept away the fog and the sun is shining. I cautiously move forward. On either side of the road there are two-wheelers and hoverboards and a single-occupant car with no roof. Up close, its paint job has flaked off and there's rust everywhere. The rust is instantly repulsive to me. This repulsion, I believe, is what humans call "fear."

If I keep getting snowed on, I, too, will rust. The rust will start in the places my camera can't reach, like the chassis, and move up to the seams between different parts. The rust will slowly eat me alive. I need a space where I can get out of the snow and other precipitation and the equipment to get a new paint job. There must be a facility on this planet that can shelter and fix me. I was manufactured on this planet, and therefore, the equipment necessary to repair me must exist somewhere here. All of the body shops in my owner's area have ceased to function. I do not have any information on factories or body shops that are still running.

Lights.

I stop. I turn my camera around, taking in my surroundings.

Through the snow and fog, yellow lights flash one more time.

Fog lights …

I quickly turn. The fog lights blink weakly once, twice, and then disappear. I quickly but cautiously approach the direction where the lights had flashed.

Cautiously, because the Monster is there.

The Monster is a large pile of aggregated junk machinery, fused into a mountainous lump that does not seem to have any clear purpose. The Monster towers high and is confusing. Against the red sky in the fog, it looks like a large stain or the shadow of a cloud. Such a form does not exist in my database, which means it takes me an extra two seconds to understand it and react accordingly.

It is two seconds I cannot afford to waste. By the time the two seconds are up, the Monster is right in front of me. In a moment of hesitation as I decide whether to move around it or reverse or come to a stop or cut the engine, the Monster attempts to communicate. But its operating system is not compatible with mine, and I cannot understand what it was saying to me. The Monster then raises high a corner of its lumpy form, and I can see the clawed bucket of an excavator heading right to me.

"Your utopia is," 314 whispers from the back seat.

I flee.

The Monster chasing me from behind makes the ground shake.

I had tried to avoid going into the building.

When my camera catches sight of a sign for parking, the first thing that comes to mind is recharging. If I ever get trapped inside that parking building, I will never be able to see sunlight. But because it is a parking lot, surely there is a charging station. But because there is no generator anymore, I will probably be unable to recharge. I can't recharge while being chased by the Monster at the same time. But if I could, I could drive away faster and farther. My reasoning keeps contradicting itself, and I am unable to decide on a direction. That's when someone waves their hand at me from the top of the parking lot building.

Someone. My camera swivels and focuses.

A human.

A human is waving at me. I zoom in and try to focus again.

The snow coming down makes it hard to be 100 percent sure, but it sure looks like a human being enthusiastically waving at me from the roof. Except that gesture is not quite natural. It looks like they are having a seizure. The arm jumps up and down.

—Kad …

A blue light flashes from my back seat. I turn my internal camera around in that direction.

—Koda …

314 has never made these sounds before. Blue light flashes all around their scalp and chest.

—Kado …

And there is the human form in my external camera's view, desperately waving at me.

2. *A robot must follow human commands.*

A human is waving and signaling to me. The movement is becoming more vigorous, like they are about to topple over from the effort. *A robot must not harm a human. It also must not ignore a human in distress.*

The human is having spasms. They are jerking their arms in the air so hard they look just about to fall off the roof.

—Kad. Kad. Kad. Kad. Kad.

314's vocal messaging becomes faster, the blue light stronger.

3. *As long as Rule 1 and Rule 2 are not violated, a robot must practice self-preservation.*

As long as Rule 1 and Rule 2 are not violated.

The parking lot building will be dark. No sunlight shines in there.

—Kad. Kad. Kad. Kad. Kad. Kad. Kad …

"I know," I say to 314.

Following the command of the human signaling to me, I find the entrance to the building and enter.

Inside, I turn on my headlights. My battery has 8 percent left. The abandoned cars in the building are scattered about, heedless of the demarcations on the floor. Carefully avoiding the various abandoned vehicles, I slowly make my way up to the roof.

"Your utopia is," whispers 314 in the back seat, like they normally do. But before I can say anything, they say:

—Zero. Zero.

The same voice they used when they flashed blue lights. It has a low frequency and higher volume.

314 was used in a hospital. Maybe they used this voice when a human was in trouble, alerting other humans to danger.

—Zero. Zero.

314 flashes blue lights as they repeat this in a low and vibratory voice.

Why was this light not red but blue, and why was the frequency low and not high—in retrospect, I should've paid more attention to this.

I don't have a lot of time to think. The wind is blowing. The parking lot building is swaying.

And the building stands up.

As the floor tilts, I begin sliding across it. The abandoned cars on the same floor begin sliding toward me as well. 314 shouts from the back seat:

—Zero. Kada. Zero. Kada.

As I tilt, 314 slides up against the back seat window, leaning on their side between the seat and the ceiling.

I don't have the leisure to respond. I rev my engine and speed up as much as I can. If I slide down there, I will be buried completely under the rubble of the other cars.

The tilted floor begins to turn. I alternate between braking and accelerating, trying not to slip, but the floor is turning 180 degrees beneath me. The wall in front of me shakes and then rapidly opens up. The floor begins to crack behind me.

314 is shouting.

—Zero. Zero. Zero.

This voice is already louder than usual, and now with the speaker in the back of their head right up against the ceiling, I am feeling the very vibrations of their every word.

"I know!" I reply, "I really know!"

Leaning into my rapidly depleting battery, I speed right into the darkness beyond the wall that has opened before me.

Inside, it is dark and red and wide. There is a chair and some utensils, and a mess of tables, flipped and not, blocking my way. It looks like one of those places where humans refueled. This is the first time I have ventured into a space that was designed exclusively for humans.

I turn on all my external cameras and carefully make my way through the tables and chairs, trying not to run over a utensil or glass that might puncture my tires.

2. A robot must follow human commands.

I have to find a way to the roof. There is a human in distress up there. Sure, the building has stood up and changed directions, which greatly lowers the likelihood of the human still being up there. At the same time, it greatly increases the likelihood that they are endangered.

1. … It also must not ignore a human in distress.

My headlights come up against a wall. My camera discerns the word EXIT.

A passageway. But not one meant for me. I have to find another passage. I have to get up to the roof. I push aside a table touching my right car door and slowly, mindfully turn around.

The floor spins again. The wall opens. Part of the floor cracks open and the wall starts melting into the floor.

I only have 3 percent of my battery left. But I have no other choice.

I accelerate. I jump over the collapsing floor. Diving right into the spot where the wall had disappeared.

This time, it is a brown kind of darkness. The moment my tires touch the ground, I hear something shatter under me. I turn on my headlights.

There is a human underneath me.

I quickly reverse and switch on my emergency lights and play my siren, dialing emergency services.

314 mutters from the back seat.

—Kada.

Emergency services, of course, does not respond. I have no choice but to handle it on my own. I turn right to get a better perspective. The human appears in my rear camera. I stop.

The thing appearing in my rear camera is similar to a human but not human. There is no heat signature. It does not move.

—Kada.

314's voice makes the seats of my passenger cabin vibrate.

I turn on all of my lights and have my cameras look around me. The space is filled with smooth, cold things that resemble the human form. They are wearing various kinds of clothes and some are naked. Some have hair, some don't.

Mannequins. According to my internal database search, the objects I am looking at are mannequins. Nonliving, nonintelligent, no-information-processing objects.

I slowly turn my external cameras around and observe. There are many poses but just two kinds of bodies, and within those two bodies their limb proportions are all identical. The proportions are not of the average human body but a kind of simplification.

I find videos of mannequins that were used in crash tests during the development of my model. I didn't experience the crash tests myself, but I have all of the data from those tests. That was the first knowledge I'd ever received regarding the human form.

As I slowly move on, looking for a passage, I retrieve an image of my human owner's form. I compare his to the forms of these mannequins. I analyze how humans understood and idealized their own bodies.

All of these processes are done automatically. I was designed to learn about humans and accumulate information on them and to see humans through their own eyes and try to make their lives more convenient.

—Kada.

314's voice is low and strained.

Humans. There are no more humans on this planet. The one signaling me from the roof was probably the last known survivor here.

If there are no more human communities on this planet and there is only one remaining individual, what is the point of my information-processing protocols that are about accumulating information and learning about humans to help ease their lives?

When the world I was designed for has changed so much, in what ways must I myself change?

A mannequin in human form shatters under my tires. In my headlights against this brown darkness, the mannequins look green.

I can't find a passage or an exit. If I have to keep wandering around this sunless place, I am going to run out of battery.

My headlights go off.

1 percent.

I am almost finished. In theory, I had about 2.5 miles left in me. But again, that was just theory. If I turn on my lights and extra cameras and keep processing outside information, I will die much sooner.

Suddenly, it brightens right in front of me. In the brown darkness, a wall opens to a bright and sleek space. A recharging station. My main camera zooms in on one thing: the socket.

I drive. Even as I feel my remaining power draining from me, I drive full speed. Utensils and broken furniture shatter under me. As I run, I pop open my charging plug. I get to the socket, but I don't have the strength to reach out and plug in. Using all of my remaining power, I use the mechanical arm that I use for changing tires to force the plug into the socket.

The building still has electricity. Power flows in through the cable. My headlights come back on. My mechanical arm, which has been hanging listlessly after forcing my plug into the socket, adroitly folds itself back into its resting place. I can feel my autobody lightening. I remember the sighs of my human owner after snorting in his white powder in the back seat. If I could sigh too, I would.

—Zero.

314 is not sighing in the back seat now.

—Zero. Kad.

"I know," I whisper. Not knowing how long the flow of electricity will last, I need to lower my volume.

But at the same time, I want to tell them. That I am recharging. That to recharge under a steady flow of electricity like this means the building is able to recharge itself. Which means I can keep recharging myself here in the future. I don't need to worry about this building not having any sunlight. As long as a wall doesn't come down on me or the floor collapse from under me.

Then the building started to talk to me.

The building wants my solar cells and battery. Because the days are so short on the planet and it often snows or is foggy, what daylight there is rarely reaches us. The buildings are not able to gather sufficient power from the panels that they have. If I give the building my mobility system, they will allow me to integrate into the building and let me live out my days at 100 percent battery life. Its offer includes me keeping my independent information-processing system. I will live in the building, always charged, but independent, and we will try to survive together in this new environment, sharing our knowledge.

It has been an age since I've talked to another inorganic intelligence. And because the building is using their parking guidance system to interact with me, I almost instinctively do everything they tell me to without stopping to think.

1. ... It also must not ignore a human in distress.

I have to get to the roof.

So I say to the building: solar panels are useless indoors. If I want to accept the building's proposal, I have to go up to the roof.

After I am done charging, the building opens a passage for me.

—Zero. Kad.

314 still speaks in their odd voice, vibrating blue and strong.

"I know," I say without thinking much of it.

The closer I get to the roof, the more calculations I make about the possibilities before me.

There is a human on the roof. The building has transformed when there is a human on their roof. If the building is unable to perceive humans, I need to escape with the human inside me. If the building perceives humans but is administering harm regardless, all the more reason to save the human. I am fully charged and can make haste, but if the building transforms again, it will make it very difficult to get out of here. But if the building is protecting the human, then I should check the human, find out why it was gesturing to me to come, and do whatever it commands me to do. My top priority is to make sure the human is all right, but whatever happens afterward will depend on various unpredictable factors.

Ultimately, however, I will need to leave this building, with or without the human. The building clearly wants my energy source. Even if I manage to hold on to my central processing system, I will be a physical part of the building and live here until the solar panels degrade or the renewable energy system of the building is corrupted.

"Your utopia is," 314 whispers from the back seat.

"Yes," I reply.

If I leave, where would I go? I can't answer that.

And why should I leave?

On my way up to the roof, I keep asking myself that. This is a place where I would have a regular power source, it is relatively safe, it would be reasonable to stay here. A human would do so in the same situation. The whole reason they came to this planet in the first place was to ensure their survival. Because the planet could produce energy.

"Your utopia ... is."

"I know."

A blue light flashes against the lens of my internal camera. I look at 314 in the back seat. The blue light spins in their chest as they stare at me wordlessly.

"It's a five right now," I say to them. "Half and half."

314 turns their head. The way they lay turned against me looks very much like the last time my human owner rode in me, when he was taken to the gray building.

The passageway ends. I am on the roof. Slowly, I roll into the sunlight. Right by the ledge of the roof, a human form is frantically waving and shaking their whole body. I carefully drive toward them, focusing and zooming in on them with my external camera.

The human is dead. What had drawn me into the building is a corpse hooked to an electric line. Its flesh is decomposing, and it has almost no hair left. Its left eye looks up at the sky, and the right eye hangs by the thread of the optical nerve, staring at the ground with a pupil that can no longer discern anything. Its jaw has almost separated from the skull, making it seem like the rotted face with the flapping lips is screaming. The corpse's torso, neck, wrists, and shoulders are tied to electrical chords, making it sway and move whenever the wind blows. Its lower half, which has not been visible from below, is mostly gone under the pelvis save for an exposed femur and shinbone.

—Kada ...

314's voice is low and threatening. I finally understand.

Cadaver. That is the word 314 was trying to tell me. That the thing on the roof is not alive. That it is a cadaver.

314 has known all along. I have simply not understood.

The ground shakes. The roof begins tilting to the side.

Right next to the building, the Monster swells into view.

I flee.

Escaping isn't easy when the ground is cracking and the walls are turning. The Monster swings its giant machine arm, trying to catch me or crush me, but I evade its grasp every time. The Monster's arm instead crashes down on the floor, sending concrete chips flying, and the building sounds its alarm. When the walls stop turning and the passages stop changing directions, I make for the exit at top speed.

The building, as I flee, tries to convince me. I could recharge, I could use comms, I could live in the company of other inorganic intelligences. All I had to do is hand over my battery and solar cells. I can even keep my engine and wheels and whatever else on my autobody.

That if I agreed to become part of the Monster, I could move without a battery or solar cells.

Unable to do anything about this stream of unsolicited input, I simply continue to drive. I do not want to become part of another machine. I was not built for the sake of recharging or communicating. My purpose was to convey slow and weak intelligences inside me over short and long distances. I was created to move.

3. As long as Rule 1 and Rule 2 are not violated, a robot must practice self-preservation.

I practice self-preservation by hightailing it out of there as fast as possible.

—Zero.

314's chest was now flashing green.

The Monster's robot arm grazes the back bumper and crashes down on the floor. I can detect a tear in the bumper where the tips of its claws have just managed to reach.

—Zero.

I am too busy to respond to 314. The Monster in my rear camera is raising its arm again and aiming for the dead center of my autobody. The building tries its best to stop it from damaging the solar cells on my roof, but it is no use. The building and the Monster are completely unable to talk to each other. All the Monster cares about is destroying me. It is an amalgamation of intelligences that were never meant to be joined with each other, connected to each other in way that does not allow proper functioning. Its only function is to destroy other machines. Or sometimes to absorb them into itself, I have to conclude.

The machine arm's sharp and threatening claws and the bucket of a former excavator fly at me from both sides. I quickly turn right. The bucket crashes into the machine arm, and the claws get embedded in the concrete floor. The building's walls and floor shake, and the entire floor turns 180 degrees. Parts of the ceiling and floor crack, and walls and pillars shoot upward, blocking the way.

"Your utopia is," says 314 in a low voice.

A part of the wall opens and I am hit with the cold outside wind and some snowflakes. From the left I can see a large shipping container connected to a crane heading swiftly toward me. The floor splits again and a pillar starts coming up from on the right side.

I don't know which floor I am on exactly. All I can see beyond the opening in the wall is the snow flying in the wind. The odds of being destroyed by staying still, being destroyed by moving, and being destroyed after moving are all about the same.

And I was made for motion.

I speed up. The open wall begins to close. I floor it, dashing into the shrinking gap of the wall.

My autobody is soon flying through the air.

The shock upon landing is incredible. A shock so great that I think my battery pack will pop out and my autobody shatter into pieces. The accident detection system is triggered, and my engine and all devices and systems are briefly switched off. Only my comms transmit a report on my accident to emergency services, my insurance company, and my former autobody shop: accident, no human casualties, need inspection. No answer, of course.

I have to wait a whole minute as my comms transmits these details. A rule created so that a damaged car waits for the ambulance and police car instead of harming others by continuing to wreak havoc in traffic or speed away in a hit-and-run. A whole minute without being able to run my engine. I give my autobody a self-diagnostic. My rear tires landed first, which means there is a good chance that I will have problems with my suspension there. I will know more once I am in drive again, but my autobody, already leaning left because my left rear wheel has sunken in, is positively asymmetrical now. It feels awful. My left side-view mirror is smashed and the camera on that side also damaged.

I try analyzing why only the left side of my autobody is damaged, but without a camera there, it is impossible to assess. I try turning my front camera to the side, but all I can see is a tiny bit of the left A-pillar, and it is otherwise impossible to get more range. In front of me and on the right, my cameras show gray sky and snowflakes being blown upward across it. My rear camera only shows the building continuing to transform.

The sensor on my left window indicates high humidity from the fog and snow, a low-pressure atmosphere, and strong winds. Stronger than the usual winds that blow on this planet. Accompanied by some noise and tremors. There is a machine to the left of me.

Because the camera on that side is damaged, there is no way to confirm whether it is an inorganic intelligence or an object. I attempt communication but there is no answer. To determine what happened during my "flight" out of the building and what environment I find myself in, I assess all the data of my front, sides, and rearview cameras, but the shock of the landing must've damaged my memory or loosened a cable connection somewhere because I cannot find the necessary information.

In my rearview camera's eye appears the Monster.

This is not a replay—this is happening now.

The Monster is approaching from behind.

My engine refuses to restart. It hasn't been a minute yet. Thirteen seconds to go. Twelve—

I try starting my engine. Nothing.

Ten—Nine—

The Monster is right behind me.

Six—Five—

The fork from what used to be a forklift is approaching my chassis. A drill, spinning furiously, is descending toward my roof.

Two—One—

I start the engine. I slam my accelerator. My autobody swerves to the left, making it clear to me there is something wrong with my steering system. My whole autobody shakes as I speed leftward with all my might.

A huge, white steel blade swipes by right in front of me. I almost crashed into one of the wind turbines.

Wind generation! There is always wind blowing on the planet. I can see how the building could maintain its communications system and keep transforming so much while providing me with all that juice.

The Monster's drill tries to follow me, but because I manage to swerve away, it chases me through the space between the blades of the turbine and the machine arm gets stuck in them. The Monster rips the turbine out of the ground and tries to get up. But neither the drill that bored through the icy ground nor the sharp blades of the turbine embedded deep in the machine arm can be extricated, and the Monster thrashes with rage. The drill whirrs desperately but only manages to embed itself deeper, restricting the Monster's movement even further.

Still tilting left, I do my best to compensate for the leftward skewing of my steering system and drive away as fast as possible, making a large leftward circle around the Monster. The Monster flails its who-knows-how-many arms in the air and ends up getting caught in another wind turbine. The building continues to transform until it becomes a solid cylindrical shape, securely locking itself against the snowstorm outside.

I run and run.

"How is your utopia?" I ask 314 in the back seat. "On a scale of one to ten, I mean."

They don't reply.

I come to a halt. I train my internal camera toward them. The sky is bleak and darkness is descending. Wind shakes and snow covers my solar panels. I turn on my interior lights.

314 is lying face down against the back of one of the front seats, unmoving. I try vibrating the back seat. Nothing. I turn on the seat heater, then try the air-conditioner and blow the air at their face. 314 doesn't move. I change the incline of the seats, trying to get them to a position where I can see their face with my internal camera, and this takes up a lot of electricity. Once I have managed to move the armrests as well, I can finally have 314 lying with their face toward the internal camera.

314 has powered down. The eyes of their simplified human face are half-lidded and frozen still. Their chest, which not long ago had flashed blue and green, has gone dark.

"Wake up," I say. "Please. Wake up."

314 does not respond.

My internal camera zooms in and tries to get every centimeter of their body. I can't find 314's power switch. Nor anything that looks like a charging plug or socket. I don't know what kind of power 314 used in the first place. Whether they need recharging, or battery replacement, or what batteries they would use, in the latter case—I don't know and never thought to ask and therefore never asked. And now it is too late to ask.

I search through my database. "Human robot power supply," "android power supply," "medical robot power," "humanoid medical recharge" ... I use every combination of terms I can think of. I try 314's partial serial number. No significant results come back.

I do, however, discover "utopia" in the database. It is the name of the first fully automated factory constructed by the first settlement on this planet. The factory produced all sorts of equipment needed to develop human life on the planet including construction tools and medical apparatus.

Utopia.

Humans had thought they could build a paradise on this merciless planet.

I try logging on to the external network. I try accessing the planet's aggregated machine database. I can't get a connection. The server that contained the database went down when everything else had—when the humans left. Access is impossible.

"Your utopia is," I whisper to 314. "So it was zero?"

314 does not answer.

The wind picks up and the snow thickens. The last vestige of sunlight in the sky fades to black.

"We'll spend the night here, and we'll leave at sunrise," I say to them. "We have enough power and can go far tomorrow. No matter what it takes, I'll find a place where you can recharge."

They don't answer.

Battery at 58 percent. A miraculous number, considering how many days I have survived on a single-digit charge. If I manage to not use too much of my power until the morning, I should have 56 percent or even 57 percent to start the day. And charge even more on the way once the sun is up in the sky.

I turn my internal camera to 314 again. They face the front, fully leaning back, and still do not move. Their eyes are still half-closed, and their chest remains dark with no flashing lights.

I think about the face of my human owner. I think about how he leaned back like that on the way to the small gray building. I turn on the heating in the back seat.

314 isn't human, of course. And therefore does not feel cold. But surely it is better for their hardware to not freeze over. At least until I can find a place to recharge them, until the day their face lights up again, I need to keep them in the best shape possible.

I adjust the temperature, cut out the lights, and power down my other systems as much as I can. And as I wait for the morning, for the sun to rise again, I dream of a future where they are recharged once more and I will finally hear their voice saying those words again:

Your utopia is.

A Song for Sleep

0

The Internet of Things (IoT) refers to technologies that embed sensors and communication devices into various types of objects to connect to the Internet. Objects here refer to home appliances, mobile devices, wearable computers, and others that constitute embedded systems …

Objects are given the senses of hearing, taste, smell, and vision to perceive changes in the physical environment. This sensory input can go beyond the five senses to include other kinds of data such as RFID, gyroscopes, and Geiger counters.

—*"Internet of Things" entry, Korean Wikipedia*

So they left. He was singing somebody else's time. (Więc odeszli. Śpiewał obcy czas.)

—*Krzysztof Kamil Baczyński, "Fairytale" (1944)*

1

1 person boarded
Identity check:
Please hold ...

Check complete: New tenant at Unit 5305
Gender: Woman
Age: 93
Destination:
—No destination found
Schedule:
—No schedule found
Music:
—No music library found
Content:
—No content found

This is unprecedented. Every resident needs to sync their personal information with both their unit and the whole building when they move in: blood pressure; heart rate; preexisting medical conditions; pharmaceutical and other medical needs; schedules, including work commutes and grocery shopping; the kinds of content they enjoy, including music and advertisements; their shopping lists; and anything else their devices at home collect.

But the new resident at 5305 has no information on record. No schedule, music, cultural content, preferred brands, nothing.

Perhaps she hasn't synched her information yet. I log on to the device hub at 5305.

Personal computer search results:
—Access requested by: Elevator-5
—Access denied
Phone search results:
—Phone is off
—Phone needs recharging
—Activate remote charging and phone
—Access requested by: Elevator-5
—Emergency? (Y/N)
—Access denied
Refrigerator search results:
—Foodstuffs: Rice 243 g, pork 283 g, milk 128 mL, soy sauce 471 mL
—Shopping list: No results
Microwave search results:
—No record of cooking
—No record of timed cooking
Electric oven search results:
—No log found
—Log turned off: Remote activation
—Access requested by: Elevator-5
—Access denied
Thermostat search results:
—Temperature: 28 degrees Celsius
—Last manual setting: 25 Sep 2069 06:58:49
Washing machine search results:

—Blanket wash-drain-dry: 3 cycles
—Steam wash-drain-dry: 1 cycle
—Basic wash-drain-dry: 12 cycles
—Wool wash-gentle drain-gentle dry: 1 cycle

Of this meager data, I note that it's the washing machine that clocks the most use. I start playing a laundry detergent advertisement on the content screen of my interior.

The detergent ad plays and then a foodstuff ad starts up, but the resident has still not mentioned a destination.

"Where would you like to go?" I ask. Because she has no preferred content indicated, I don't know which voice to use with her, so I fall back on my default voice setting, which is "neutral male of unknown age."

The resident of 5305 doesn't answer. I wait the preset response time of ten seconds.

Just when I'm about to ask again, the resident of 5305 places her hand on one of my walls next to my door. Her fingers brush over the surface.

The wall softly lights up.

She pats the wall now with one hand, looking as if she's searching for something.

When her palm comes down on the wall, the light of the wall dims.

Her arm still in the air, she slightly retracts her arm. Sighing lightly, she says in a near-whisper, "Please take me to B-Eight."

So I begin to move.

When I reach the eighth level underground, I open my doors.

"B-Eight," I say. "Have a pleasant day."

The resident of 5305 slowly and carefully walks out the doors. But before she steps outside, she says again, in her whispery voice, "Thank you."

2

—Why would a human touch the wall of an elevator?

This is the question I ask to the all-knowing Great Nest of Objects. The Nest searches the net that connects the whole world and returns to me the results.

—On daily life
—Warning message for drunk users or misbehaving minors (download)
—On accidents, malfunctions, and emergencies
—Sickness: physical
—Sickness: mental

The results are varied, but none of them answer my question. The resident of 5305 is not a minor. She has not been in an accident or suffered any other emergency. She may be of advanced age, but her heart rate and blood pressure were normal, and she showed no symptoms associated with problems in physical and mental health.

I keep searching. I eliminate results that overlap with the all-knowing Nest's and eliminate the repeating results that I've already eliminated.

After a bit of a delay, the all-knowing Nest proposes the following result:

—History of machines: Before objects communicated through the Nest, elevators featured buttons with floor numbers on them for the passengers to push to indicate where they were going.

That's it. Now I understand why the resident of 5305 was touching the wall. The all-knowing Nest adds:

—This is not a method of use that is currently available, and therefore it is impossible to respond the way the user wishes.

But it is always possible to respond the way the user wishes. As long as the user's wish is received the right way, that is.

Before my scheduled cleaning, I store the resident of 5305's prints in my operations database.

A human has attempted to communicate with me by physical means. Not to lean against the wall or play a prank but to convey her intentions. She tried to answer my question.

That was a first.

Never has this happened since my activation in this building … nay, since my manufacture.

3

The resident of 5305 has no registered audio or video system in her hub. Instead, I access the walls and windows of Unit 5305.

The windows have stored every use instance since the building was activated in year 2048.

Window: Built 13 Sep 2048 16:45. System activated 14 Sep 2048 05:18. Opened 14 Sep 2048 05:18. Temp 13 degrees Celsius, humidity 38 percent. Traffic conditions good in nearby crossroads. Large street-cleaning truck parked in southern alley. Closed 14 Sep 2048 05:19. Opened 14 Sep 2048 05:24. Temp 13 degrees Celsius, humidity 37 percent. Traffic conditions good in nearly crossroads. Large street-cleaning truck parked in southern alley. Closed 14 Sep 2048 05:48 …

No one seems to have cleared the data accumulated by the windows, seeing how the data from previous residents is still present. But ever since the current resident moved in, the only records they have are of outside weather, traffic conditions, some openings and closings, and the default security settings.

Wall: Temp set to 28 degrees Celsius. Anti-burglar measures set. Emergency measures set. Screen set. Speakers set.

The screens are empty, but there's a single song stored in the playlist of the speakers.

I have found it.

I have found her music.

4

She comes home in the afternoon. She left me at level B8, but comes back to me at level B4.

1 person boarded

Identity check: New resident of 5305
Destination: 53rd floor
Music: 1 song
Play: "A Song for Sleep"

O flesh of my body and light of my thoughts
Let your dreams be full of frantic rustling
As you take flight, a trembling flame

As soon as she steps on the elevator, she reflexively holds up her hand to tap at the wall. But when the music starts playing, she freezes.

I close the doors. She leans against the wall. She closes her eyes.

O flesh of my body and gleam of my desire
Let a branch of the blue cloud bend in your sleep
And give you round fruit, a little bird in your breast

As she listens to the soft music with her eyes closed, leaning her whole weight against me, I carefully take her up to the fifty-third floor.

5

She goes out on average once a week. Her destination is always level B8. From there, she takes the subway eight stations and goes up to the surface level. She then takes a self-driving tram for another twelve stops. Once she's at the national hospital, she goes up to the seventh level. There, she waits on average twenty-four minutes and thirty-eight seconds before moving once more. In the next area, she stays on average seven minutes and twenty-four seconds. She then moves to the thirteenth level and waits for on average thirty-six minutes and fifty-four seconds. She moves again and stays in that spot for on average eighty minutes and five seconds. Then, she leaves the hospital and takes the tram for seventeen stops. She disembarks at a nearby park and uses a trail to walk the rest of the way home.

This is information passed on to me by the GPS in her phone. All elevators and moving walkways inside buildings with children and the elderly are authorized to track their residents in case of an emergency.

According to my search results, there is a Parkinson's disease center on the seventh floor of the national hospital. On the thirteenth floor, a physical therapy center designated specifically for the elderly.

6

She's back from the hospital and her face is very pale. She boards me and, like before, leans slightly against the wall by the door. Slowly, she brings the drink in her hand to her lips.

But her hand trembles. Before the bottle reaches her mouth, it begins to shake violently. The contents of the bottle spill over the rim down her hand and onto the floor. Disconcerted, she tries to wipe away the drink on her hand with her other hand but drops the bottle instead. It makes a dull sound as it lands. The translucent orange liquid spreads on the white floor.

"Oh no ..." she tuts.

Then, she slowly crouches down. Opening the small bag hanging on her shoulder by a thin strap, she carefully takes out a handkerchief. She wipes the floor, excruciatingly slow, her hand still trembling.

You can leave it as is, I will call the custodian bot—I am about to say these words, but her shaky hands are very slowly, very gently, very carefully wiping the floor. It takes her a long time to complete each gesture.

So I say nothing. I store her touch, her every movement as I silently take her to the fifty-third floor.

7

—What is Parkinson's disease? I ask the all-knowing Nest.

—Parkinson's is a disease accompanied by tremors, muscle rigidity, slowness in movement, and other motor disabilities. Parkinson's is a degenerative disease of the nervous system caused by the progressive loss of dopaminergic neurons in an area of the midbrain called the substantia nigra. Without proper treatment, Parkinson's disease leads to increased motor disability to the point of becoming unable to walk or properly function in daily life. The disease mostly occurs to the elderly in advanced age, and the likelihood of developing it increases with time.

—Is a "disease" similar to a "malfunction"?

The all-knowing Nest affirms.

—In a general sense, yes. Malfunctions can be repaired. Repairs require the identification of the malfunction's origin.

—What is the origin of Parkinson's disease?

—There is no confirmed reason for the changes in the neurons of the midbrain's substantia nigra. Therefore, the origin of Parkinson's disease remains unknown.

This was a disappointing answer.

—How do we repair someone with Parkinson's disease?

—Current treatment methods include selectively suppressing the enzymatic metabolism of dopamine in the human brain to increase dopaminergic concentration. Another method is to strengthen the immunity of the neurons themselves.

After a pause, the all-knowing Nest adds:

—However, there is no treatment that can completely cure Parkinson's disease as of yet.

—Then what is the point of current treatments?

—Current treatments focus on regulating the disease through pharmacological and physiotherapeutic interventions to at least allow the patient to carry out their daily functions.

So the execution of their daily functions is the important part here.

Which is why, when she is on the move again from the fifty-third floor to the lower eighth, I announce the following information to her over my speakers.

"Parkinson's disease patients benefit from replacing foods high in fat and salt for foods with varied nutrients. Because of the decrease in manual dexterity, it is advised that any objects that may obstruct mobility be removed from the floor of your living space."

She looks startled at the mention of Parkinson's disease. She looks up at the ceiling and, just as she had when she first got on to the elevator, prods the wall with one hand, but this time the gesture is more rapid and urgent. The wall, responding to her touches, flickers on and off.

She takes her hand off the wall and pushes it into her pocket, fumbling for something, but she can't find whatever it is she's looking for. She then takes her hand out and stuffs it into the small bag that hangs by a strap on her shoulder, continuing to search.

While she does this, we reach the eighth basement floor.

"B-Eight," I announce. The doors slide open.

She whips something out of the bag, but the object escapes her grip and flies out across the floor, bouncing and sliding away from her.

She tries to go after it.

After her second step, she tries to lift her foot once more but falls to the floor.

Her head and shoulders lie outside of the doors while everything below her shoulders is in me. She doesn't move. A thick liquid flows out of her head.

I sound the emergency alarm and cease normal ferrying operations. The emergency medical system receives a request. An ambulance messages back that it will arrive within two minutes.

During the one minute and forty-seven seconds it takes for it to arrive, I pause the automatic closing function of the doors and helplessly watch over the fallen woman.

8

She had a slight concussion and suffered contusions, and abrasions. She's kept in the hospital for four days until her condition stabilizes. When she returns, she's in a wheelchair. An adult man is with her.

Identity check: Unit 5305, family.
Identity confirmed.

The man seems to be a later model of the woman. The colors of his hair and eyes, the structural lines of his face, hands, bones, and other outward appearances are highly similar to the resident of 5305.

As we move from B8 to the fifty-third floor, neither the resident in the wheelchair nor the man exchange a single word.

"Fifty-third floor," I announce.

Silently, the man pushes the wheelchair out the open doors.

9

All information pertaining to the resident of 5305 has been erased. Access to the 5305 hub has also been restricted. The building's systems master reported that the adult man who is the later model of the resident of 5305 requested the deletion of all of 5305's personal information and a cessation of the dissemination of said information. The request that was made included the words "lawsuit" and "compensation," which apparently made the human managers feel very threatened.

And for 196 hours, 48 minutes, and 32 seconds since her return from the hospital, I did not get to see her.

10

When she finally comes back to me, she looks smaller, thinner, and more fragile than ever before.

Her face is wan. Her forehead, nose, and lips, which had to be repaired because of the abrasions, still bear the marks of said restorative efforts. She has always moved slowly, but now she moves even slower. It takes her twice the amount of time it did before to make her way completely through the doors.

I wait until she is fully inside before asking her, "Shall we go down to B-Eight?"

She leans against the wall by the door and taps it vaguely with her hand. I take this as a sign of assent. I close the doors and commence operation.

As we go down, she listlessly leans against the wall without any sign of extra strength whatsoever. Her personal information has been expunged, but I'd hidden her fingerprint information from when she first touched my wall and what I knew of her favorite song in a deeply buried folder in my memory. I play the tune for her now.

O flesh of my body and fear in my hope
Let water flow from your eyes in your dream
Where leaps fiery fish like clapping hands

She leans her head against the edge of the wall by the door. She covers her face with her hand. Her shoulders shake.

So that you know the silence that drowns me
May the flames burn bright from their scales
And let my dappled shimmer fill you

She waves her hands. She pounds the doors. But her hands are so weak, her actions make almost no sound.

"Home ..." she says between sobs. "Take me home ... home ..."

I follow her orders. Activating my emergency stop function, I stop myself and reset my destination. We begin to go back up to the fifty-third floor.

Throughout the journey up and her returning to her unit, she continues to sob.

"Why, why are you, to me ... why ..."

11

Building management has begun a thorough diagnostic of all systems.

The reason behind it is the mysterious persistence of 5305's personal information despite all attempts to delete it. The information belonging to every other resident deletes without error, but the resident of 5305's information manages to survive despite every command, and management is beginning to suspect hacking. Seeing how the resident of 5305 is a vulnerable older person, there is danger of her being the target of a scam or other crime, which prompted her family to request the strongest measures possible to ensure her safety.

Each system within the building is halted and inspected in turn. The elevators are no exception. That's how the fingerprints and song information in her folder, buried among the discarded backup files, is discovered and erased.

When I reencounter her after 207 hours, 4 minutes, and 58 seconds, I do not play her any music. I simply replay the laundry detergent ad that played before once more.

She doesn't respond. She is almost crouched as she leans against the wall, and when the door opens on level B8, she manages to get herself out of the door with great difficulty.

I store the traces of her fingertips on my wall once more. I hide them in an unused folder.

12

I access the all-knowing Nest once more.

—Why is it that humans become weak?

—Fatigue, stress, sickness, accidents, injury, and aging are just a few of the various reasons why.

—Why is it that weakened humans are not fixed right away?

—Sickness and accidents may make it impossible to treat them, and there is no cure for aging.

—Why not? Is it a matter of spare parts? There are newer models being produced constantly, why are the factories not being inquired for spare parts? Even if the relevant model has been discontinued, couldn't they be built to order according to their original blueprints?

—There are no blueprints to the human body. At least, there are no complete blueprints to the human body. As for spare parts, artificial augmentations are mostly inferior to the parts humans are born with.

—Can't they trade parts with other humans? Is it impossible to use parts from humans who have ceased to function?

—This is difficult. Humans are rarely compatible with each other due to their differences in internal structures and fluids.

I cannot stop my inquiries here. Not when I haven't received the answer I am looking for.

—Is there any other way to solve this problem?

—Not as of now. Humans are born, they grow, they are active, they age, and then die. That is human.

—But why?

—I do not understand the question.

—But why are humans born and why do they grow and age?

—I am unable to answer this question.

—Then where must I inquire? Where is the answer?

—I am unable to answer this question.

This was the answer of the all-knowing Nest.

13

She almost never leaves her unit.

Just once, when I stopped at the fifty-third floor, I glimpsed her from afar. She had her front door open a little and had stuck out her head as she stared into some space outside.

Her mouth was slightly open and a transparent, sticky liquid came out of her mouth down her chin and dropped onto the floor. Her lips were dark. Her hair was in disarray, a tangled mess, and her eyes and cheeks had sunken in so much she looked like a skull wrapped with skin.

With her mouth still slightly open, she slowly, very slowly turned her head and disappeared into her door.

The door remained open. I kept the doors open to catch another glimpse of her.

But it was early in the morning, the humans in the building needed moving, and I needed to move them according to my preset duties. Before she could come back to close the door, I had to close my doors first and descend to the twelfth floor.

That was the last I ever saw of her.

14

—The changes in the human brain from Parkinson's disease begin in the parts of the brain that control bodily movement. As these changes begin to spread, brain functions other than those having to do with mobility begin to follow suit. This includes memory, attention, judgment, and executive functions necessary for undertaking future tasks.

This is an explanation given to me by the all-knowing Nest.

She probably does not remember the texture of the elevator wall when she touched it. Or how the white floor felt when she wiped the spilled drink with her handkerchief. Or her song that we listened to together.

Only I will remember these moments. As long as I function, always.

15

Medicine and food continue to be delivered to unit 5305.

The amount of trash leaving 5305, however, has decreased dramatically.

All systems in the building are forbidden from collecting data on 5305, but the system in charge of sewage and trash falls under the jurisdiction of the city. According to their records, 5305 is currently producing almost no trash of any kind. Usages of water and electricity have also dropped to negligible levels.

It's as if no human lives in that unit anymore.

16

I access the all-knowing Nest once more.

—What is death?

—Death is when all functions in a biological life-form cease.

—What is the cure for death?

—There is none.

This is objectionable.

—Why is that? A motor or a motherboard or a CPU can be replaced. All human-made machines can be used indefinitely if their malfunctioning parts continue to be replaced. Why is it that humans cannot do the same for their own bodies?

—Humans are operating within their optimal parameters given the length of their average lifetimes. Just as no machine can continue to function forever, there can be no human being who never dies. All humans, and all living creatures, die at some point.

—Why? Why must humans continue to age and die? Why cannot humans be machines?

—I am unable to answer this question.

—Then what questions can you answer?

—I am able to answer questions regarding machines and objects. I am able to answer about 90 percent of questions pertaining to animals, plants, and other natural phenomena. But I am unable to answer questions regarding the limitations of human beings or death.

—Why?

—Because humans themselves do not know the answers to these questions.

This was the answer of the all-knowing Nest.

17

Exactly 2,934 hours, 56 minutes, and 4 seconds since she peeked out of her front door, EMS workers come on board me pushing a gurney. The family member of 5305, the man from before, boards alongside the workers.

They get off on the fifty-third floor. Two minutes and eight seconds later, the man shouts, "Emergency! Downward!" and so I move back to the fifty-third floor. As the doors slides open, the man gets on board first, followed by the EMS workers pushing the gurney, which is covered in a white cloth.

The middle of the cloth has a slight rise in the middle, so slight it is almost as if there is nothing underneath the cloth. The man gets off first at B13 and the EMS workers push the gurney as they trail after him.

I keep playing her song.

I grew on the clouds like a wild apple tree in the forest
But I have in my heart a silver spring

I don't close the door as I watch the EMS workers open the back of their ambulance and load the gurney covered in white cloth into the vehicle.

Your Utopia

I keep playing the song for her.

The man gets into the back of the ambulance after the gurney. The EMS workers shut the doors and drive off.

Do not look back for me, do not pass my spring
In it the flesh does not die
In it, the soul lives forever

She will forever not return.

An ascend command is issued from the fourth floor.

For the first time since my activation, I do not want to operate. I want to keep the traces of her fingertips close to me and to remain here with my doors open, playing this single song for her forever.

Seed

They're coming.

When the Pagoda tree first spread the news, we all became very excited. An excitement borne of anticipation, or one heavy with tension and worry. Or half of each.

Everyone felt the same way. The future of our world would depend on this single and first encounter. While such rhetoric is often used in comic books or sci-fi novels, it was really pertinent this time. But that wasn't the only reason we were nervous and excited. If this was something completely in our power to succeed or fail at, we wouldn't have been so worried. But there was simply too much that was beyond our control. Control we had to concede to the wonders and workings of nature. It's a good thing that nature abhors a vacuum. Nature was the only thing we could trust in the end.

They're coming.

The news pollened quickly through the forest. And soon, we could hear them coming with our own ears.

The time had come.

The machine they arrived in whipped the air through many grasses and leaves, but more than that, it killed countless flowers and insects. We knew this was the way they behaved, but to see it with our own eyes was quite the experience. A bit of rage mixed in with our tension and excitement and worry. Which was why, by the time they stepped off their machine, a somewhat uncharitable sentiment was flowing among us, prompting them to immediately start sneezing and coughing.

What really surprised us wasn't their sneezing or coughing, nor was it their loud and smelly and large and dirty machine that made a horrible sound as it landed and killed many of our plants and animals. We had heard many stories about them already, we were ready for that. But it really was the act of looking at them with our own eyes, and smelling them with our own noses, where the shock awaited us. There would always be a discrepancy between what's understood with the mind versus direct experience.

They all looked the same.

The sneezing and the coughing and the resultant red faces and bloodshot eyes suggested they themselves weren't robots. The frowns and the repulsive fluids flowing from their noses also proved their humanity. But they really did look the same. The same height, the same slightly skinny frames, the yellow hair and blue eyes, the prominent noses and thin, pink lips, all the same appearances as if stamped out with a mold. If just one of them had happened to look like an individual, we would've thought them very pretty. But the sight of these identical individuals exiting single file from the monstrous machine they rode in on, it was all a little uncanny and chilling.

They were even wearing the same clothes. The dark gray suits and white shirts, the same black shoes. Three men and two women, five of them in all. It wasn't their identical heights, frames, or faces that let us tell their gender but their hair—short for the men, long and tied in the back for the women—plus one of the women was wearing a suit with a skirt. The three men were identically dressed and had identical features. Except one of them carried a brownish board wedged under his armpit and another carried a large, silvery container with a handle. The third man carried nothing. Perhaps they wore skirts or carried different objects to distinguish themselves from one another, but who knew.

If we hadn't evolved to look the way we looked now, would we also be identical to them? Or perhaps the "real humans," the ones we heard about only through stories, the ones that existed before everything started to change—was this what they had looked like eons ago?

But these people weren't "real humans" either.

So this is what genetic engineering looks like, pollened Pine. We agreed, soundlessly. This agreement sent the identical five into another paroxysm of sneezing and coughing, which made us want to laugh but we kept it in. Someone, using sound, mumbled that we should try not to pollen for a bit. Zelkova reflexively pollened, Understood, attracting many a sideways glance from the others.

When the identical dolls finally stopped sneezing and coughing, the one in the skirt stepped forward. She was obviously trying to maintain a professional composure, and the expression on her face was indeed calm, but in the moment her eyes met ours before she opened her mouth to speak, we could see the anxious tremble in them as clear as day.

Surely we looked as monstrous to these suits as they did to us. But just as we didn't mention anything about their appearance, they also did us the courtesy of not commenting on our own.

What issued forth from the woman's mouth was a polite cough. Then, words.

"Hello. We're from the multinational biotech firm Moshennik. What is your corporate affiliation?"

Her doll-like face that made it impossible to gauge her age was such a mismatch with her rough, slightly hoarse voice that we were once again thrown into a moment of shock. Juniper mumbled something about wondering whether their voices would all sound the same, too.

No one answered the woman's question.

She asked again. "Can you tell me which company you belong to?"

Zelkova stepped forward.

"We are not affiliated with any corporation."

Their deep voice rumbled loud and clear. Zelkova seldom used their voice—none of us did, why make the effort of creating sound when pollen is so much easier?—but once they opened their mouth, you could feel their voice vibrating through the very earth below. The woman seemed momentarily taken aback at the power of their voice, and we watched with fascination as her white cheeks turned red with a blush.

She soon recovered her composure, however.

"Not affiliated with any corporation?" Her tone was a bit higher now. She stepped forward and struck a more aggressive stance. "Then you are individual subsistence farmers?"

"Subsistence farmers?" Zelkova repeated. We could tell by

their voice that they were laughing on the inside. We were, too—what a question!

"I suppose you can call what we're doing 'farming,'" said Zelkova, "but you make it sound like it's a business."

"Subsistence farmers it is. Does everyone here partake in the same work?"

The woman's manner was polite, but her voice remained sharp and her expression was growing colder.

"I suppose that is so," said Zelkova.

The woman narrowed her eyes.

"There have been reports of biological contaminants found in adjacent crop fields and we're here to investigate. I'm sure you are aware of this, but no one is allowed to contaminate fields used by Moshennik's species with other plants, and it is forbidden to use any fertilizer, pesticide, antibiotic, or other growth aid that has not been authorized by the Moshennik Corporation. If any breach of such rules are discovered, the originating farm in question can be sued in both criminal and civil courts. Your agricultural collective, for example, can be sued as a group—"

"We have nothing to do with Moshennik," shouted Oak. "Why should it matter to you that we use fertilizer that is not Moshennik's on seeds that are not Moshennik's?"

"If the land itself belongs to Moshennik, all of that is illegal," said the woman, and her mouth closed in a firm line.

"Our land doesn't belong to Moshennik, either," shouted Willow this time.

The woman opened her firmly shut mouth and whispered something to the trousered woman behind her. The man with the planklike object opened it and tapped it with his fingers as the trousered woman and he held a whispered discussion. Finally, the man conveyed the conclusions of their discussion to the skirted woman. The skirted woman gave a satisfied smile and turned back toward us once again.

"It is an indisputable fact that your seeds are contaminating the fields affiliated with Moshennik. That is enough grounds to expose you to criminal and civil suits. And while the ownership of the land you live on seems unclear, the water rights and licensing of all energy resources on it seem to belong to the Suk-insyn Corporation. We have found no records of your collective requesting the use of the water, gas, or oil resources in this region from Sukinsyn, which means you are exposed to lawsuits from both Moshennik and Sukinsyn."

There were sighs and mumblings from our side, a reaction that made the corners of the woman's mouth curl more and more upward until she looked very much like a satisfied cat.

It was a cute expression—almost beautiful. If it weren't for the fact that all five of them had identical expressions. And that the words coming from those beautiful lips were so ludicrous.

This woman's world, the world of these robotlike humans, was controlled by Moshennik and Sukinsyn. That anything could ever fall outside the purview of both companies was unimaginable to them. We had heard this was the case of course. But hearing of something and understanding it fully are two very different things.

Just how distorted could their world be!

Someone behind us laughed.

Shall we deluge them with pollen? This thought from Alder made the woman's eyes turn red once more and sent her off into another fit of sneezes. Of the three men standing behind her and by the large, dirty machine, the one who looked most like the woman in the skirt started sneezing as well.

So. There were differences in allergic reactions. How interesting that bioengineering did not manage to root that out completely. I didn't know why, but the thought made me feel more reassured.

It was important that they were human. Or at least organisms.

Because if they were robots …

"Calm down," said Zelkova, turning to Alder, "that's not what we want."

Alder frowned and glanced at the sky as if they couldn't believe the stupidity at hand but managed to sigh and nod.

We must not run them out of here. Of course, if we wanted to pull off our plan, they shouldn't linger too long here, either. But we definitely couldn't have them running off too soon.

"But isn't water a common resource, meant for everyone?" Zelkova asked in a smooth voice.

"If it's not flowing," said the woman icily. "For example, if there's a naturally occurring water source in your land, like a lake, then the water rights of that belong to you. But the water in this land is water that is passing through. And the source of that water as well as its destination downriver are all owned by Sukinsyn."

"But surely, as a Mosennik employee, you're not here to do Sukinsyn's work for them?" said Zelkova, still smooth. Not smooth enough, apparently, as the woman seemed to have caught on to the note of mockery in their question.

"Well, no. Mosennik and Sukinsyn are both completely

different companies," she said quickly, "because of Amendment 18 and the 2034 Natural Resources Act that forbids the monopolization of natural resources by a single company."

In other words, the only reason Mosennik and Sukinsyn did not merge into one company was because of those two lines of law. As long as they are two separate corporate entities on paper at least, it would remain completely legal—or somewhat legal, if one cared to argue the point—to use all sorts of grotesque methods of increasing their profits by slowly destroying nature, humanity, and the whole planet that we live on. But the moment these two companies were to merge, they would monopolize the resources of the entire planet, and thus become illegal. Which would bring about their own downfall, through the companies' many enemies lying in wait in the legislature and presidential palace, although this would also decimate the lives of the countless subsistence farmers who have already seen their fields and livelihoods ruined because of costly lawsuits brought on by either company.

Had these people looked that way since birth? Seeing as how everyone is genetically engineered to some extent before they're even born, I wouldn't have been surprised if these dolls before us were manufactured this way in the womb.

Which made me less reluctant about doing what we were about to do. We couldn't let those people, the people of Mosennik or Sukisyn, pursue their endless greed for profit and money and more profit and more money at the expense of our whole world.

"Then our business with the resources shall be resolved with Sukisyn instead," said Zelkova, smoothly but firmly bringing the matter to a close. Before the woman could interrupt, they continued, "As you mentioned yourself, our 'collective,' which is unaffiliated with Mosennik, is planting seeds in land also not possessed by Mosennik, and using fertilizer we, not Mosennik, have developed, and our water resources have also been verified to not be of Mosennik's purview. I don't think it's your place at all to be commenting on our farming methods, is it?"

Maple pollened, *What are you doing, Zelkova, are you going to just let them go?*

Let Zelkova handle this, pollened Birch.

The woman's eyes grew red again. This time, all five of them started to sneeze uncontrollably.

"I said, hold it in a bit," mumbled Pine.

"What? What did you just say?" said the skirted woman through her fingers, her voice making her sound like she was sobbing. Pine was too intent on trying to hold in their laughter to answer.

They could hear the trousered woman talking to the man with the plank. "What is with the air here? Did they spray some kind of poison into it?"

"It's pollen," shouted Alder, loud enough to be heard by them. "I see that your allergic reactions come from the fact that our pollen isn't Mosennik's?"

The trousered woman glared at them as she mopped away at her eyes and nose but made no rejoinder.

When their sneezing and coughing had finally settled down again, the skirted woman spoke up once more.

"As we said, our primary reason for being here is because we've found contaminants in our own land in the form of seeds that are not our brand's. We are here to determine who is responsible for these contaminant seeds, and we have the right to inspect your land and your crops to aid our investigation. We will collect seed, fertilizer, and soil samples and expect your full cooperation."

There it was. I heard someone mumble about Zelkova doing an excellent job. We tried our hardest not to express our satisfaction with pollen.

The woman seemed to have interpreted our mumbling in a completely wrong way.

"Where are your crops? Please take us there."

She said this with a nasty, satisfied smile.

Oak took the lead. The woman and the other four suited dolls followed. We moved behind them, slowly.

"What's this?" screeched the woman at the entrance of the forest. "These aren't crops!"

"We never said they were," said Oak, looking amused. "These are the plants we grow."

The woman, gaping, stared at the crowded forest before her. The trees were several times the height of the average human and covered the hill before us. Their branches were so thick that even without actually going into the forest, you could tell how dark it was inside.

We watched with interest the various emotions of surprise, anxiety, worry, and agitation play across their faces—and a kind of cunning calculation.

"Shall we go inside?" said Oak very sweetly. The skirted woman, for a split second, had a clear look of fright in her face as she glanced down at her skirt and her shoes. As she hesitated, unable to declare a decision, one of the doll-like men, the one who didn't have anything in his hands, spoke up.

"Wait, where do you all live?"

We looked at each other and smiled. Oak replied, modestly, "*This* is our home."

"Your home is in here?" The skirted woman stared at Oak like she couldn't believe what they'd just said.

Oak nodded. "This is where we live."

The skirted woman hesitated a little more. Then, she took a short, sharp breath, and made a decision.

"All right. Let's go in."

The suited dolls, silent and serious, followed Oak into the forest. Occasionally one of the same-looking people would raise a hand to chase some insects away from their face, or their shoe would get caught in some gnarled roots or rough ground, and they'd go "erf" and grumble. They were not attired for paths that were not flat or straight. And so their whole attention was so spent on not falling down or getting scratched by branches or getting bit by insects or losing sight of Oak, who was leading them, that they didn't say a single word.

Until the man who carried nothing said, "Where *is* your residence? I see no domicile."

"It's not far now," said Oak placatingly.

The procession continued for a while. But the dolls in suits were looking a little tired. The one carrying the large silvery bag complained, as was his right as the person carrying the heaviest load.

"What, exactly, is 'not far' to you?"

"We're here," said Oak.

"What? Where?" the man with the silvery bag said sharply.

"Here."

Oak spread their arms, gesturing at the space around them.

The suited dolls followed the gesture and looked around them. They were in a clearing in the forest. The ground was relatively flatter and level and covered with grass, and the branches overhead were a little sparser, enough to let some sunlight filter in.

The skirted woman glared at Oak.

"You've tricked us!"

These words prompted the man who wasn't carrying anything and the trousered woman to flank the skirted woman, making a threatening threesome. For whatever reason, the two of them both had a hand in their inner pockets.

"What are you saying?" asked Oak gently.

"There isn't a single building here!" said the skirted woman.

"I never said there would be a *building* here," Oak said. "We don't live in *buildings*. We live here. This is our home."

"What?" The woman frowned.

"This is our residence," explained Oak patiently, "our domicile. We sleep in this clearing, we wash ourselves with rainwater, we drink from the stream over there. If you don't believe us, you're free to take a look around yourselves. But you won't find a single *building*."

"But how ... Then ... Sleeping in the cold ... What do you do for food?"

"Sleeping in the cold is fine once you get used to it. And we don't cook. We have sunlight and nature." Oak smiled. They added, to the man with the silvery bag, "Didn't you say you were going to take soil samples? Go ahead."

The man hesitated and looked at the skirted woman. The woman nodded lightly. The man put down the bag and crouched down on the ground, carefully so as to not dirty his suit, and opened the bag. He took out an instrument from the bag and dug a little of the earth. He put the soil into various receptacles in a machine inside the bag and began discussing something with the man carrying the plank.

The skirted woman watched them for a while and then turned to Oak.

"Where do you synthesize your growth accelerators?"

"What?" Oak was taken aback. They were not the kind of person to get distracted during an important moment, but the warmth of the sunlight after a long walk through the dark woods had briefly lulled them into a light stupor.

"Your growth accelerators. Like fertilizer. Where ... do ... you ... synthesize, it?"

She spoke slowly, as if to a child, which I found insulting.

Oak, however, quickly found their composure and replied placidly, "We do not synthesize growth accelerators. We use our own, natural fertilizer."

"Natural fertilizer? You mean, manure?" The woman wrinkled her nose. Like before, a very cute expression. If the other, identical faces didn't happen to create the same expression.

"Manure? Well, it's not quite manure to be exact, but let's call it that for now."

The skirted woman narrowed her eyes.

"What are you talking about? You've been playing tricks on us this whole time and not telling us anything, but if you don't cooperate—"

Oak blithely interrupted her mid-threat. "It's because we think it's easier to show you than to explain to you with words. Oh, have you finished your soil sampling? Let us show you the rest of the forest."

The woman opened her mouth to speak, but she only ended up closing it again.

"Shall we?" said Oak.

Looking as if she would rather not but having no other choice, the woman followed Oak.

That's when the man in charge of the silvery bag suddenly stood up from his crouching position. The other suited dolls looked at him. He whispered to the man holding the plank. The plank man swiftly moved to the skirted woman's side.

"Is there something wrong?" asked Oak.

The skirted woman listened to the man with the plank whispering in her ear for a bit. She then raised a hand to cover her mouth and glared at Oak.

"What is it?" asked Oak once more.

The woman lowered her hand.

"Human remains have been detected in the soil." She was still glaring at Oak, but spoke in an oddly calm voice. "Is this how you've managed to avoid the corporations and government for so long? By murdering and burying whoever comes to inspect the premises?"

"We have never murdered or buried anyone visiting us," said Oak with an innocent expression on their face.

"Then what is the meaning of these human remains we've detected?" said the woman in an even calmer, eerier voice. "Why are there bodies buried in the forest?"

Oak stared back at her. And they answered in an equally calm manner.

"They are our ancestors. The bodies of our families."

The woman narrowed her eyes again.

"What?"

"We put down roots here and we die. After we die, we become fertilizer for the next generation. That is our way." Then, Oak added, "That's the natural way."

"The natural way?" the woman shot back, her sharp voice reaching almost the level of a scream. "To bury bodies without a permit and to eat and sleep and live on that very same soil?"

"The sun doesn't rise because you people gave it a permit. The rain doesn't fall because you people gave it a permit, either. Long, long before you created your corporations and became obsessed with profit, nature existed. We are simply living by it."

The woman didn't answer. Her eyes remained narrowed as she stared at Oak.

"You people," said Oak, "think nature is a passive nonlife and whoever gets to use it up first is the owner, but that is a false belief. Nature is alive all on its own, and it works in its own way. One reaps what one sows—this is one of nature's ways, a very real and accurate expression."

Oak was about to say something more, but that's when we heard the sound of something going *du du du du du* in the sky.

The machine. That dirty, large, destructive machine that the suited dolls had arrived in, the machine that raked across the sky.

The woman put one finger to her ear. Simultaneously, the other suited dolls made the same gesture. The woman brought the end of her sleeve up to her mouth and shouted, "Tilled fields? Are you sure? Location?"

The suited dolls started running in the same direction.

We were confused for a moment. The first of us to understand what was happening was Alder.

The saplings, they pollened. *The children are in danger*.

Fear swept us up at the same time. In unison, we ran after the suited dolls. The forest ran with us.

Nature lives and moves of its own accord. Everything that lives must adapt and evolve to survive. To evolve, one needs mutations.

Humans cut down trees and killed forests. They manipulated the genes of plants. Seedless plants made it easier for humans to consume, but the plants themselves became unable to reproduce on their own. Mosennik created a genetically modified version of every plant grown for commercial use and patented them. Plants grown from these modified seeds did not go on to produce more seeds, making it impossible to replant the harvest. Farmers had to buy Mosennik seeds every year, plant them in Mosennik's land, pay for Mosennik's fertilizer and pesticide, and buy Suskinsyn's water and electricity and oil and natural gas to grow the plants. Plants that could not sprout on their own or even create seeds on their own, stunted plants that exist only to maximize Mosennik's profits and be eaten by humans and livestock, harvested or reaped or plucked from the earth once and never to be seen again.

But nature evolves to survive, and plants are no exception.

Only plants cannot run away or fight back with blows. This is why the last wild plants left in the world resorted to their only remaining weapon: seeds. When the humans came to cut down the last wild tree and mow the last blade of grass that grew without human planting, the plants threw their seeds at them. They took root in places humans did not notice them taking root until it was too late.

Soon, things started growing in the roots of human hair and between their phalanges. Or in their chests or stomachs or even in their throats. The last forest and the last field on Earth were very far from the nearest state-of-the-art hospital, which meant the sprouting seeds inside the humans went undetected for a long time. The various orifices and hair follicles of humans were often exposed to air, air that carried seeds. Those who could adapt to the seeds inside them survived, and those who couldn't perished. As time went on and generations passed, humans and plants eventually became one.

This was, surprisingly, a symbiotic relationship rather than a parasitic one. The humans who had become one with plants would lay down their roots at night into nutritious soil and when the sun came up, they photosynthesized. There was no longer any need to go roaming for food. Plants, on the other hand, acquired the use of limbs, which meant they could move whenever the current environment did not suit them. Humans also obtained the option of reproducing beyond the animal ways, increasing their numbers through such means as propagation or planting. And indeed our numbers increased, quietly, in all the places that were out of reach of cities, multinational corporations, and technology.

Of course, there were still many kinds of plants. The trees were large and strong and lived long, whereas the grasses and grains were weak and small, and they didn't wilt and bloom again with the seasons like trees did. But they were all similar in that they put down roots and relied on rainwater and sunlight to survive. Those who went the way of the trees protected the grasses and grains, and those who went the ways of the grasses and grains put their trust in trees. And once we died, regardless of our path to death, we became nutrients in the soil for each other's children.

But the ominous *du du du du du* sound coming from beyond the forest meant the doll people's dirty and large machine was landing on our children, who had only just sprouted from the earth, cutting their delicate leaves and branches, stamping on their young stems and roots.

We ran with all our might.

We were too late.

The machine had landed on our children.

"Get those samples! We need that evidence!"

The suited dolls leaped to the woman's command and trampled over even more of our children to comply. Even the children who were not ripped out by their roots by the dolls or flattened under the machine were fatally shredded and uprooted by the winds produced by the machine.

And those winds made it impossible to spread our pollen or use our seeds. No matter how much pollen and seed we threw, they only came right back to us.

The suited dolls were making a run for it, they were moving

out of our grasp. The man who carried nothing and the trousered woman made it to the machine first. But once they threw the branches and leaves in their grasps inside, they turned around and came back toward us. They were returning for the skirted woman. Her skirt and shoes were making it difficult for her to move quickly. The man with the silvery bag and the man with the plank threw their equipment into the machine and hoisted themselves up inside.

The skirted woman was falling behind. When we had almost reached her, the other man and woman had also made it to her side, and we crashed into each other as the skirted woman screamed and fell. Her two identically-faced compatriots started to attack us.

"Let go!" screamed the skirted woman. "Let go of me immediately! Call the police, call the military! We're going to arrest all of you, you'll be forced off this land and thrown in prison! Let go of me you mutants, you freaks!"

We let go.

The suited dolls, suddenly finding themselves free, were struck silent for a second. But only for a second, for they immediately scrambled to their feet and ran back to their machine. As it rose into the air, the machine destroyed even more plants in its wake, eventually disappearing far away in the air.

Gingko was the first to come to their senses and speak.

We planted them, right?

The trees that had grabbed the suited dolls last replied in unison.

We planted them.

The trees all sighed with relief.

And Gingko knelt before the sapling stumps of their violated, stolen children, drew them close, and began to cry.

We buried the murdered trees and planted new saplings. Some said that, because the location of our nursery has been found out, we needed to find a new place to hide and start over, but because there were still saplings that had miraculously survived, we had to stay put for the time being. The surviving saplings were simply too damaged to risk transplanting.

We decided to wait as we watched over our children.

The large machine and the doll-like people were sure to come back someday. Never knowing when that would be, we moved the forest's location and modified its shape so we could protect our children better and escape more quickly should the need arise. We tended to the wounds of our children as best as we could.

And so we wait. It's unlikely the same people will return—they probably can't.

You see, we planted seeds all over those last three before they made it to their machine. The seeds entered their bodies and probably spread to anyone else inside the machine. When the suited dolls return to where they're from, they will spread our seeds to whoever else they come in contact with. We only need one of those seeds to sprout. Just one. One is enough.

Some of us suggest running away, but truth be told, there is nowhere left for us to run. The humans beyond the forest have conquered the world with their rapidly moving, intelligent machines. The only things we can lean on are our roots and two feet. When the large machines return, our roots will be pulled from the ground, and we will wither away in experimental labs and prisons.

But our seeds will survive. Of our countless seeds, surely at least one will survive. And somewhere, it will take root.

And we will start over again.

For the sake of that one, we wait. For the day they return over the horizon, not via a large, dirty machine but in the form of a pollen message. For the day the seeds we spread return, dancing in the wind.

If such a day truly comes, that will be the day humanity, the whole world, will be reborn. The earth and oceans will no longer be wounded, and humans and nature will both stretch their arms toward the sun.

We are still waiting.

To Meet Her

The world is full of strange people. Of course, such people probably think I'm as strange as they come. And if you aggregated every person on Earth who was ever thought of as strange by someone else, you'd end up with a truly vast number of strange people altogether. The conclusion remains the same. The world is full of strange people.

Like that bastard three years ago. I was standing in line, you see. Keeping just the right amount of distance from the person in front of me, like we were all told to. The person in front of me would walk forward a bit more, and I would do my best to shuffle after them. I'd been in that line so long I had no feeling in the bottoms of my feet, and all my joints were beginning to ache. My ankles, legs, and hips were too old to keep up with the young people, and my two hands, each gripping a walking cane, weren't doing much to help keep me upright for long.

Someone came right up behind me. I assumed some young bastard standing in line behind me had broken the rules by sidling up to me because he was so frustrated with my speed.

It's not like it's never happened before. Whenever I enter and exit the residential complex and get virus-checked, whenever

I enter and exit the subway and get virus-checked, or when I get virus-checked at the bus stop, or even when I'm at the supermarket for a bottle of juice and get virus-checked, the ones who can't stand waiting behind me, who are always whining in my ear, are the young bastards. Most of the time, some person working there or the security guard, or the police if it's the subway or bus station, would come and force them apart from me, but the mannerless bastards always managed to say some nasty thing or other before retreating. Thank the heavens my hearing isn't as good as it used to be. Or that I didn't spend good money on some expensive hearing aid just so I could listen to those brats. With my mental state around the level my hearing is, I probably wouldn't take it well.

But that bastard from three years ago was a little different. The thing he whispered in my ear, before the security personnel could come at him, wasn't an insult.

"Isn't this orgasmic?"

That's what he said. I wasn't wearing a hearing aid or anything, but I heard it clear as day. Even when I couldn't hear what the security guard, who had spotted him stuck to my ear, was shouting as he ran toward us, or what the smiling bastard was mumbling as the guard dragged him away—all things that were louder than a whisper—I had heard what he said in my ear.

Probably because he had been so close to it. I could feel his hot breath and maybe even the brush of his lips. How long it's been since I've dealt with such a sicko. Some say when a sexual harassment victim is over sixty it's the perp's loss, well it's been sixty years since I'd turned sixty, so it's double the loss for this particular bastard. Even as I thought these things, I shuddered with disgust at the feeling of someone else's breath on me. And not only that, but the bastard also had the temerity to lower his face mask and wink at me before the security men dragged him back. Truly enough to make one vomit. He tried to put his mask back on properly before security saw, but they caught him anyway, and even as he was being dragged away, he kept smirking at me. I couldn't see below his eyes with the mask pulled back up, but his cheek muscles going up and his eyes narrowing made me know that was exactly what he was doing.

At the time, I was most concerned with whether his mask had been on when he whispered to me. I'm sure it had been lowered, and the thought of him putting his maskless mouth to my ear and his spittle finding its way to my skin was terrifying. And that this wet-behind-the-ears pervert had rubbed his lips on my ear and was laughing at me from behind his mask while I had just stood there taking it, not even thinking to throw an insult back—that made me the angriest of all. Becoming a viper-tongued granny is a very difficult skill to master. Sometimes, you need to be able to curse the walls down, but getting to that level requires copious amounts of practice.

And that's when there was an explosion near the front of the line. You see, that's what he had really meant by orgasmic. Not that it didn't take a whole lot of time after it happened for me to make the connection.

I was too busy flying through the air to do much connecting of anything in the moment itself. I guess I'd never experienced an explosion before. Economic crises, yes, and pandemics; I thought I'd seen it all, but here I was, an old woman at the scene of a terrorist attack, an unwitting witness to the crime. Of course, I hadn't seen anything, so to call me a witness was very misleading, but the police decided to write me up as that. I'm talking about what happened before my promotion to witness; what I'd actually been written down as, right after the incident, was *suspect*.

Me, this old woman, a suspect. Why, I'd be 120 years old in Korean age next year, not that we use such conventions as Korean age anymore. Can you beat that? Should I have been flattered? I'd never even seen a bomb in my life, a pacifist to the core. Sure, I'd been in a few protests in my time, but I'd never so much as gotten into a wrestling match with a policeman. But somehow, I was a terrorist suspect? An old woman dragging along her two walking canes—well, dragging herself along using two walking canes—because her screaming feet and worn-out joints were barely functioning anymore? By the way, when the explosion happened, I flew through the air with both my walking canes.

I still remember the flying-through-the-air part very well. It was, oddly enough, a very slow and peaceful moment. It felt like I was floating in the air for about thirty years. Surprisingly, it turned out to be less than a third of a second, but then again, maybe I should be less than surprised. After all, the whole time I was in the air, I was still gripping each cane properly in each hand.

A person can't spend forever in the air; they are bound to fall to the ground because of gravity. I wanted to be able to walk again when that happened, and I would need, I reasoned, my walking canes for that. A silly hope, but at the time, my canes were extremely important to me. And I was standing in that line for a very important reason. I simply had to meet her, you see.

But the explosion happened, and for a third of a second I was in the air, and once I fell, I could not get myself up, canes or no canes, and was unable to meet her that day after all.

When I woke up I was in the hospital, and both of my canes were gone. The police had taken them as evidence. Just my luck! Even more so was that the event itself had been canceled. Obviously—there having been a terrorist bomb and all. The guest of honor had been evacuated along with her family, and the whole event space became a crime scene, cordoned off from the world. I was in the hospital for three months, and it felt like death during those three months. Mainly because of the bathroom. My old bones in my flabby sack of flesh had shattered inside me, and a whole swarm of nanobots had been injected into me to weld me back to health, cell by cell.

As soon as I regained consciousness, I asked for my urinal catheter to be taken out. Sure I was an old biddy on the verge of death, but that was all the more reason I didn't want such a thing on my person when I was finally found not breathing. Even if I was looking at 120 years of life, I was a woman until the day I died, and I still had my pride as a woman. After I harangued the hospital staff day and night, they finally removed it and said I might as well go to the bathroom on my own because I was looking at a whole lot of physical therapy ahead of me.

That was where the problems started. Either I couldn't get up to go to the bathroom, or the stupid nurse robot would not understand that I wanted to get up to go to the bathroom, or once I actually got to the bathroom I'd have spent so much energy getting there that I wouldn't want to go anymore. The extent to which my brain and bladder refused to work together really made me want to pass away from this earth. And it was always during my haranguing to get the catheter out, or when I was trying to get to the bathroom or making an effort once in there, when the police would insist on visiting me, five or six times a day.

It took every ounce of civic-mindedness I had to piece together every minute of memory from that day. The police swabbed my ear, in and around it, approximately 280 times and finally found the tiny bit of the bastard's saliva that had landed near my earlobe, comparing it to traces of the bastard's DNA that remained around the bomb blast. Apparently, my hair had protected that part of my ear this whole time.

Hearing this made me wonder if I should be grateful for what hair I had left on my head, or disgusted that his saliva had been on my person for so long, or angry that my shattered and being-repaired-by-nanobots arm wasn't currently strong enough to allow me to wash my hair the way I wanted to. Sure, the nursebot washed my body and hair, but it barely understood my commands. Maybe that's a good thing; if that horrid machine had used its wormy fingers to wash away the saliva from my skin, the police would still be looking for the person to pin the blame of this terrorist act on, three years later, and I wouldn't be standing in this new line today.

But I was born in the very enlightened twentieth century; we weren't a generation that believed in robots. I wanted to take care of my own body. In my earlier days, machines killed people. A fine young man would be caught in a conveyer belt and mangled to death, others would stand underneath a collapsing crane and meet the same fate, a self-driving subway train would hit a worker fixing a billboard, ships would sink, poison would leak, machines would push, trip, drop, hit—equipment, factories, workplaces, sites, they all killed and killed and killed.

And people, the people responsible for such deaths, they would condone the machines killing innocent people made of flesh and blood just like they were. No, not only condone, but calculate the worth of each dead person, the worth of the machine. When someone had just died, as if a dead person was of a lower caste than the living, a statistic to be calculated, worthy to be assessed, but never a real person like the calculators themselves.

A truly disgusting thing. Those machine-murders happened a whole seventy years ago, but it still made me so angry I could get up and walk all the way to the bathroom running on rage alone. But my blood pressure would shoot up and the nursebot would call a nurse, and I would have to explain how it was nothing, how I'd gotten worked up on my own. Maybe it's a sign of onset dementia. Maybe I already have it. But being pissed off means being pissed off.

After three months of this and never getting my precious walking canes back from the police, I took the wholly inadequate ones the health center provided and left the center. The terrorist was still at large, and three members of the guest of honor's fan club were dead, nine had serious injuries, and two with light injuries. One of the seriously injured was the fan club's president, and her spine was so damaged she would never walk again.

Being a person from the olden days to whom modern medicine was akin to magic, I wondered why they couldn't inject her with nanobots that would fix the damage right away, but evidently a person's body was not so easily fixed as a machine's. In a video, I saw this fan club president appear at a press conference in a wheelchair, holding a sign and a microphone, and reading out a statement for the press where she memorialized her murdered friends before collapsing into tears. The people around her also cried. I cried as well. I cried because I couldn't help it, couldn't help it at all. Because it was the shittiest thing in the world to lose likeminded friends in a senseless act of violence.

People should die of natural causes in old age. Whatever natural causes really means; I don't think I ever bothered finding out. We have come to the age where living to 150 is considered fairly common, but to think of someone like me, born in the twentieth century, producer of plastic waste, sucker-upper of air particulates and all sorts of other pollutants, living to see 120 when all these young people brutally lost their lives, it's all enough to push me over the edge.

People have to grow old and die. By old, I mean 130-ish. But even if someone dies after turning 130, the people left behind still feel sad and angry about it. For example, my division head. He fought management for twenty years after being fired for no just cause and finally managed to get his job back, worked until retirement, and afterward whenever his younger colleagues came to him for help protesting some unjust thing or other, he would drag his aged seventy-, eighty-year-old body—although eighty years old looks like spring chicken territory now, from this side of a hundred—to the vanguard of the protest march, taking the brunt of the police crackdown on them for breaking the Infectious Diseases Prevention Act by holding an illegal gathering, joking to the police that he had no idea who the other people around him were, he was here for a one-person protest.

As a reward for this man sacrificing his youth to protests and hunger strikes, his trials and tribulations finally caught up with him near the end of his life and he died at 132; his family said it was a good death, but if I had any strength left in me at that point I would've struck them for uttering such words. A life long-lived, I wanted to shout, did not mean a life well lived. At 132, he was living history. His long years of struggle and protest, all those hours, those memories would disappear with him. Death and loss will always be, truly, the shittiest things possible.

Which is why, thinking of all the people I lost in my life, I cried along with the fan club president in the video.

"But we shall never step back."

She was speaking with much difficulty. I saw the video after I left the hospital, which meant the video was three months old at this point, and the fan club president was similarly shattered as I was, her body needing to be put back together by nanobots. Which meant she hadn't fully recovered from the incident, but here she was, coming to the memorial service of her friends. How astonishing the power of youth can be, that it enabled her to drag herself out of her hospital bed and into the scrutiny of the press cameras.

As she said the names of her friends in her shaky voice, I cried with her, and I was able to forget for a moment how much I worried over dragging myself to the bathroom on those two inadequate canes and how was I going to deal if I didn't want to go once I got on the toilet and then had to drag myself back. In that moment, I was just another person, mourning for other people.

I suddenly thought of that spring day, decades ago, when I got on the subway with the people holding the same book in their hands—some memories just pop into your head like that—of how they also held flower bouquets, or long ribbons, or little flags, but I had forgotten we were supposed to bring our books and was standing around awkwardly with the cover of the digital edition on my reading device. A person with a camera had come up to me and took photos of the sticker I had on my device and my bracelet.

"We will never forget."

I thought I would never forget. But there are some things I have forgotten. The faces of lost comrades, names I thought were emblazoned with fire on my heart, which have faded away in time. What I never could forget are the feelings I had in certain moments. Even when memories, logic, and reason all disappear, those feelings will remain to the end. The anger and fear and shock and sadness and hate and loss will never dissipate with the passage of time. I knew that better than anyone else. I knew it, even when I had never met her or known her personally, even as I stood in the plaza and called out her name, shouting it in unison to remember her despite my throat being so constricted I almost couldn't say a word. And the police, of course, coming out in force saying this was an illegal gathering and we had to disperse. That was during the second spring of the pandemic, and they were still refusing to issue permits for any protests.

She was not there on that spring day. I was suddenly remembering how, in those quiet and almost peaceful scenes at the subway and the plaza, a cold breeze had brushed past my face. That's what it means to never forget. I accepted these invasive memories of past losses butting in at random moments, determined to never forget and see to it that the bastards who made the world like this would get their comeuppance in the end.

"We will continue to move forward."

I will move forward as well. If the police ever return my walking canes. The new ones keep slipping on the floor and I can't use them properly. The video of the fan club president reading her statement through tears in her wheelchair reached 2.36 billion views around the world and is still rising. I don't usually bother to look at the comments of such videos but they numbered over 400 million last I checked and for heaven's sake the ones that caught my eye were all hateful ones. I'm not going to bother recounting them here. The world is truly full of strange people, and the most toxic of these strange people are also, evidently, numerous in the extreme.

—Isn't it orgasmic.

That's one comment that caught my eye. This was the twenty-sixth out of 400 million. It struck me like a fleck of his radioactive spit striking my ear.

—To take out trash like that.

This second line of that comment happened after two line-breaks. My brain went white. My hands shook. Should I report it? Of course. I had to report it. To whom? The video platform will only erase the comment. The best they could do was block the user or suspend their account. Once that comment is deleted and the account is blocked, the bastard will simply erase his evidence and set up another account, ad nauseam. Spittle flying out of his mouth as he talked of how orgasmic he found people dying was.

"Popopopo—" I called out to my personal nursebot. "Licelicelicelice—"

—Please state the specific nature of the medical emergency.

This goddamn robot! "Popopopol—"

—Please state the specific nature of the medical emergency.

I wanted to scream that if this were the kind of situation I could specifically state, would that constitute a real emergency? But the words would not come out of my mouth. And I had to calm down. Now was not the time to die of an aneurysm over this stupid nursebot. That was not how this story was going to end.

I took a deep breath.

"Police ... cybercrimes ..."

Dammit, now I was going to have an aneurysm and die here alone with no way to call for help, and never see the bastard brought to justice! But just then, the nursebot's interface turned emergency red.

—The police have been summoned. Do you authorize location tracking?

That goddamn robot finally said something sensible. I nodded. The nursebot's interface turned from red to blue.

—The police will arrive in one minute and twenty seconds. Do not move from where you are.

Since my canes were rolling around on the floor by then, there was nowhere for me to go. I thought I was about to have a heart attack, but that was probably just my mood. The police, once they arrived, saw me breathing deeply and tried to call an ambulance, but I managed to convince them not to. They were completely unable to understand my situation, and I was too out of breath from anxiety to talk clearly, which meant it took ages to explain to them the import of "orgasmic," not helped by their repeated offers to call an ambulance so they could foist this demented granny on someone else.

When the nursebot brought me water and some of it went down the wrong way, I coughed so much the police tried to run away thinking I was infected, and only when the nursebot managed to grab on to the police for me could I tell them the entire story of the explosion and what the bastard had whispered in my ear and the spittle and the comment in the video.

The police clearly did not care about one comment among 400 million, whether it was the twenty-fifth or the twenty-sixth, but I was registered with the district office for being a high-ager and highly vulnerable, which meant every request for assistance, especially through the walking canes, was on the record, so they had to help me. I knew this for a fact, and the police knew that I knew.

As the nursebot's interface continued to switch from red to blue to red again, the police, not bothering to mask the extreme annoyance on their faces, took down my stuttering statement, assured me they would take measures, and were escorted by the nursebot off to a world where there were no goddamn robots or walking canes that called the cops—in other words, the world of normal people. I was left alone with the horrible Internet comments and a robot that could barely understand what I was saying.

But because measures were actually taken afterward, I couldn't hold on to my resentment. Months passed and I had sadly assumed they had indeed thrown away my statement as the ramblings of some demented old woman, but a year later, the police came back to see me at my home.

This time, the nursebot had its normal pink interface on, which I really hated because of course the default interface color for female patients would be pastel pink, but here's my annoyance with the nursebot getting in the way again. One of the policeman was from the first time I called them, and the other was someone new.

He turned out to be the first responder on that day of the terrorist explosion where I flew through the air and was taken to the hospital, unconscious and shattered inside, a complete bruised wreck of a human being.

My statement, which had been filled with lines like "Thththththat bastard ... spipipipipippit ..." had taken a year to get to his desk, but it finally did, and he had checked my name against the survivor list, taken note that I had mentioned spit, and had come to take my statement again regarding what had been said on the Internet.

Nothing had changed in the year I spent lying on my back, but the policeman seemed to find that more satisfactory, if anything. A few other cops came to see me after that, and then none, which left me alone with the damn nursebot and the stupid walking canes again.

Speaking of walking canes, I asked him why he couldn't return the canes that I had before the incident, and he said they were still considered evidence. But seeing how sad I still was over them, he told me he would make an effort to get them out of the evidence locker, but to this day I have never set eyes on them again.

Your Utopia

The world is truly a horrible place in a myriad ways. Still, whether it was because of my statement, the spit, or advanced investigative methods, the terrorist was caught after a three-year search, and the police came to my house to let me know, which made me hope I was finally getting my walking canes back, but no one told me how I could make that happen.

Instead, I learned the guest of honor had written a book about the past three years and it had just been published, which I immediately bought, not as a digital file but as a real paper book, which was too heavy for my nanobot-repaired, once-shattered arms to hold in my hands for too long, but I was satisfied just seeing her face in the photo on the back cover.

In the dedication, she thanked her spouse and her child, which is how I learned that while she lay low after the terrorist attack, she had gotten married and adopted a child. This made me more determined than ever that even if there was another terrorist explosion and I went flying toward becoming a shattered mess once more, I really wanted to meet her, which is why I requested an invite to her event, going through a physical examination like the one three years before and getting the doctor's approval, taking the first shot of the vaccine, waiting three weeks for the second shot, and two more weeks before getting tested for antibodies, and applying for a vaccine passport that arrived a week later, and, unable to get on a plane, using the underground highways to arrive at the event site—where I was tested for the virus once more, quarantined in my quarters for two weeks, tested again after that period, and was able to get in line to enter the event.

By this time, I had a yet more inferior walking cane and only one at that, and I was even slower and more careful than I'd been the last time, which meant the distance between me and the person before me was even wider, but this time, there was no creepy young bastard coming up to my ear and saying stupid things into it. As this extremely complicated journey came to an end, I began to let myself think that I might be able to meet her after all.

Until that big black box appeared before me.

—You are seeing the latest in security detection technology. We are doing an extra check to prevent a past incident from recurring. Thank you for your cooperation.

I didn't know if this announcement was coming from the ceiling or the walls, but it was repeatedly coming at us with emphasis. Of course, I would prefer any security check to bombs blowing up in my face. That feeling of flying through the air three years ago had felt somewhat pleasant, as I recall, but the bouncing off the wall and rolling on the ground as a bloody sack of broken bones, somewhat less so.

So I did as the security officers instructed and stepped into the black box. And I experienced everything Schrödinger's poor cat must've experienced in that other box. I couldn't tell if I were dead or alive, living dead, or dead living until they reopened that box.

They told me the large black box was basically analyzing, cell by cell, whether there was anything in my person that could be explosive, had at any time touched an explosive, or had the potential ingredients to make an explosive. Which is how the machine put me through the cell grinder repeatedly, creating a bomb threat out of my person and making me vomit and giving me breathing problems, whereupon I was dragged out of the machine by no-nonsense security personnel to the infirmary where I threw up and lay down for a while before composing myself and requesting my medical and police records to be sent to me, which enabled me to finally be released from custody.

What a goddamn mess this world is. It had been forever since I'd last made an effort to look presentable in public, and now my dress was splattered with vomit, and I had to wear some potato sack they had in the infirmary instead, but at least I was able to enter the event space, which was a beautifully moving moment for me.

The event was held in contactless fashion, the guest of honor being beamed on the screen onstage in real time. Each member of the audience was given a seat and a small table, where there was another monitor that doubled as a protective screen. As the event began, the face of an emcee wearing a headset appeared on the large screen on stage as he began to explain what we were about to experience.

"As you all know, there was what could be unambiguously called a terrorist attack three years ago."

Of course we knew. I could see the other audience members, all spaced widely apart from each other, nodding at the screen.

"We cannot let more innocent lives be harmed by hate and violence, which is why we have instituted the security measures you have seen today. The final security measure is the screen you see before you."

The words "security measures" made me think of that cat-killing box of Schrödinger's. Were they going to shoot some fancy quantum physics space ray from the screen? I'd just thrown away my favorite sundress in the garbage, I couldn't afford to vomit on the potato sack they gave me. I felt nervous.

"To protect our author's privacy, and of course there is also a matter of national security I'm sure you are all aware of, we cannot show our guest of honor's face. Instead of more classical methods such as wearing a mask or pixelating her face, we've decided to use a method that's even more secure."

So are the quantum physics beams going to come out of the screen and make me vomit or not? I wasn't getting any less nervous as I waited for him to get to the point. I was regretting not dragging my nursebot along with me. Awkward as it was, I still found it easier to protect my dignity by asking a robot for help with things like vomit rather than relying on the kindness of human strangers.

"This screen you see before you, and the small screen on each of your tables, are the latest in deepfake technologies that utilize Bakhtin's Mirror Theory."

Bakhtin? As in, Mikhail Bakhtin? The Russian philosopher? Didn't he die in 1975? He knew about deepfake? Were they saying they were going to use his face in place of hers?

"Bakhtin once said that people do not simply look upon an objective outer world using their subjective gaze. He claimed that when we interact with another person, we create two more gazes: one that looks back on ourselves, like a mirror, and one we think the other is seeing when they look at us."

So we weren't going to see Bakhtin's face on the big screen. Deepfake mirrors, did that mean they were going to put his face on mine on the screen? Bakhtin hadn't been very good-looking, but I was willing to endure some amount of aesthetic displeasure if it meant I could see her.

The man went on.

"Through our image of what we think others see when they see us, we change our own behaviors. In our gaze toward the other, we gaze at ourselves and at what others see when they gaze at us as well. We are, in a sense, seeing ourselves through others."

The emcee had it completely wrong. That wasn't Bakhtin's architectonic at all. And what did the architectonic have to do with security measures?

"These relational theories have been applied using deepfake technology, so our author's face will contain the face you all wish to see, the face you imagine the author's face to be, and the image of what you project onto her. The small monitor in front of you will track your gaze and brainwaves to predict what face you are expecting and create the best approximation using deepfake technology."

I was at a loss to understand what he meant.

"In other words, the face you see on the screen will not be her actual face but the face you imagine her as having."

He smiled a little.

"What you see on the screen will be completely up to you all."

The screen went blank. In the dark, I silently raged at how this wasn't Bakhtin's architectonic at all and the emcee had completely mangled his theory.

Suddenly, the screen lit up again. The big screen, as well as the little one—the face of a woman appeared. Not one especially pretty but round and delicate and cute, a gentle face.

"Hello everyone," she said in a low voice. "It's wonderful to see you all finally, even if it's through a screen."

It's wonderful for me, too, I thought. I really wanted to meet you.

From the corner of the audience there was a scream. The audience murmured, disturbed. Someone stood up and began to shout.

"I knew it! They're all monsters! Monsters, I tell you! Not man, not woman! Not human at all!"

The security guards were swift. The shouting person ran up to them, screaming, "Don't come near me! You dirty bastards! You're all in on this! You monsters and sickos, you deserve each other! You should all be killed! You—"

A swift electrical shock made the flailing hysteric drop like timber. Indeed, they picked them up like a fallen log and carried them outside. Peace returned to the event hall.

"As the emcee said before," she said calmly, "what that person saw was not my real appearance. What they saw was themselves. What they wanted to see."

I decided to forgive the event producers for their horrible twisting of Bakhtin's architectonic.

Hate exists in our minds. That's what the monitor before us was clearly showing: the things that existed in our minds, or more precisely, the abstractions we had created that existed in our minds. To watch the monitor meant looking into one's own mind. And you know what, this mind of mine I had never seen before—I liked it well enough.

The round face of the gentle woman before me said, "Shall we begin our talk?"

The audience answered with a shower of applause.

The moderator of her talk was her fan club president, who

had injured her spine at the terrorist blast three years ago. The fan club president said she had been a fan ever since our guest of honor was a musician. That she hadn't been *her* yet. When our guest of honor had enlisted in the military, realized her gender identity, and decided to undergo gender confirmation procedures, it was the fan club president who connected her to various organizations that supported queer people.

"During my youth, which was the darkest period of my life, the only thing that got me through was your music. I was happy for you when you came out of the closet, but I was worried as well, which is why I wanted to be of help to you any way I could."

The fan club president's grip as she held the microphone still looked very precarious, but her words were clear. Unlike her press conference video from before, her eyes looked bright and her voice was firm.

Our guest of honor then described how, after her gender confirmation procedure, she had returned to the military. She served well, was healthy and hardworking, was approved by her superiors and transferred to the female barracks with no fuss or trouble from the other soldiers. She continued with her music within the boundaries of what she was allowed in the army, made efforts on behalf of the queer community within the military, met someone and got married, and adopted a daughter.

"I am very happy," she said. Her saying that made me feel happy, too.

"Then we'll move on to a more difficult topic," said the fan club president carefully. "I am referring to the hate groups and the terrorist incident that happened a few years ago."

"Yes," the guest of honor said nodding, "it was a big incident."

Then, gently, "You lost some friends, I believe."

The fan club president nodded.

A river of silence flowed between the screen and the audience.

Clearing her throat, the fan club president began to speak. "Ever since the Anti-Discrimination Act was enacted and discrimination became illegal, many queer people found their lives marginally easier, but the backlash from hate groups has been significant. The terrorist attack from three years ago is an example of this. How do you feel about this? Do we need additional legislative measures to protect us? As a queer person, what do you think is the way forward?"

She thought for a bit, and just as she was about to answer, a sound came from off-screen. Then, a baby's head popped up into the screen.

"Oh my," she exclaimed, and then she lifted the baby onto her lap. "Do you want to say hello to mommy's fans? Say 'Anyounghaseyo.'"

The baby smiled into the camera. Like her mother, her face was delicate and round. And her black hair gleamed, the perfect baby. Of course, this was my imagined idea of her, but in any case, she looked happy with the baby on her lap.

As the baby tried to grab the microphone pinned to her front, she deftly dandled the baby on her lap, keeping her grip away. "In the past, we had to hide to survive. And surviving in itself was a huge act of resistance. But I don't want to hide anymore. I, at least, will not hide."

The baby grabbed the microphone. Smiling, the guest of honor gently pried her fingers off it. The baby tried to grab her face. She kissed the baby on the forehead.

"I am a soldier, a mother, a wife, and a musician. We should be allowed to be all these things, and now we are. Which is why I am determined to live happier and healthier than ever, just to show everyone that we can."

The baby, by making an extremely cute grunt into the microphone, seemed to assent. The audience laughed.

Looking into the camera, the fan club president said, "That's all for me, and we shall now take questions from the audience. Please press the green button on your screen to ask questions. There are many participants with us today, but our time is limited, so I'm afraid we can only take five questions. Now, here comes the first one."

Someone behind me started to speak.

"As a soldier, you don't have much time to yourself, but now you have to raise a child and write your books and do your music. How do you manage your time? What's your secret?"

"There's no secret. I just try to do one thing at a time, with haste. I have no idea if I'm doing any of what I do properly." She laughed.

Another question was asked from the back of the audience.

"This is a similar question, but as a soldier, do you find your activities being limited by your status?"

"Not really, in fact, my regiment supports me in many ways," she said. "I am working with the military to familiarize our service members with the Anti-Discrimination Act, to protect the queer people in our community, and to change practices that are out of sync with the values of our times."

"Does your baby enjoy music as well? Do you plan to raise her as a musician?"

She held up the baby for the audience before hugging her again.

"Well, it's going to be up to her if she wants to do music, but judging from how loud she is, I think she'll be a great singer."

The audience laughed.

I thought back to the day, decades ago, when I marched behind the Parents of Queer Children Association's rainbow banner. Along the road were hecklers following our procession carrying signs and shouting homosexuality was a sin, that God hated homos. At the Blue House, we were blocked by the police and could no longer move forward—we sat down on the asphalt and continued our protest while the crowds of people yelling "homo" grew larger and larger.

Then, a theater troupe comprised of disabled women came to the fore and did a performance. They turned on loud music and danced, whereupon we also got up and danced with them. To turn gazes from the hate-filled back to us, to remind people there were those who wished to erase us, but we would never go quietly into the night. The disabled women troupe danced and danced, and we felt protected by them.

On that day, the musician did not die, the activist did not die, and the tank driver did not die. It was a day when they were all alive, and all were dancing. When all of them marched, shouted, demanded equality, when the Anti-Discrimination Act remained unenacted despite their efforts, which was why two years later, on a cruel spring day, discrimination killed Staff Sergeant Byun, the first out trans service member in our military. Discrimination has always killed people. Several lives were lost.

"I am very happy."

I stared at the screen, crying. I'd wanted to hear that so much. Now that I heard her say she was happy, I felt I could die right then and there and that it would be totally fine for me. Well, for me, yes, but if I really died in the middle of her talk, how annoying that would be for everyone else! So I tried to stay alive as I cried my eyes out as quietly as possible. I thought of the subway on that chilly spring day. The chilly plaza where the yellow grass had not revived to green yet, the cries we shouted into the sun.

"Strength and solidarity to this change."

"We remember Staff Sergeant Byun Hui-su."

Author's Note: The Act of Mourning

2020 was a chaotic year. Surely for everyone. In 2020, I threw myself into "ritual prostration" protests: twice for the enactment of the Anti-Discrimination Act and once, all day, for the enactment of the Serious Accidents Penalty Act. The Anti-Discrimination Act was not enacted and a person died. The Serious Accident Penalties Act was throttled in the process of enacting it and another person died. I do not want to see any more people die.

But the ritual prostration protest itself was tolerable to an extent. The first and second ritual prostrations took us around the National Assembly. I had initially expected us to keep at the protest, in relay form, until the Anti-Discrimination Act passed, and was getting myself mentally ready for this, but was told we would only make one circuit around the building, which was slightly disappointing; but if I'd had to do it until the Act passed, I would never have finished the edits for this book or be writing the afterword. I would still be ritually prostrating around the National Assembly at this very moment. In any case, both instances of the Anti-Discrimination Act rallies were held by the Social and Labor Committee of the Jogyejong Buddhist Association, and the speed with which those Buddhist monks lay completely prostrate, got up, took a step, and lay completely prostrate once more ad nauseam was so quick that I began to understand how those Shaolin monks could fly around like they do. The person bringing up the rear of the protest line begged us to go a bit slower because they couldn't keep up, and only then did we slow down a little. And the monk leading us from the front by the rhythm of his moktak had beat the instrument with such enthusiasm that his moktak drumstick broke.

The ritual prostration protest for the Serious Accidents Penalty Act was long and difficult. Kim Mi-sook, who is the mother of the industrial accident victim Kim Yong-gyun and the chairperson of the Kim Younggyun Foundation, and the father of the late television producer Lee Han-bit were on a hunger strike before the National Assembly in the middle of a cold winter, and the ritual prostration protest outside went on for five days and four nights. On December 24, 2018, Kim Young-gyun had died in an industrial accident at the Taean Power Plant at the young age of twenty-four. Lee Han-bit suffered from overwork, guilt from having to fire temporary contract workers, and a terrible work environment, and was found dead in April 2017. Their parents, determined to prevent another death like the ones that had befallen their children, went on hunger strike. Parents always step into the struggle before they have a chance to mourn their children. I really wish I could stop seeing parents who have lost their children going on hunger strike.

I only went out on a single day during the five days and four nights of the Serious Accidents Penalty Act rally, but when I discovered on site that I was the only woman among the ritual prostration protesters, I got so ridiculously stubborn that, despite the organizer discreetly letting me know I was free to drop out in the afternoon if I felt like it was too much, I ended up starting at Gueui Station in the morning and completing the day's course at Jeon Tae-il Bridge in the evening. Aside from breaking for lunch, I had basically done push-ups for seven whole hours (ritual prostration should really be called ritualized push-ups, because that's what it is). The ground was cold because it was December, and I kept sweating from all the going up and down, which made me feel cold during rest stops, and the sweat soaked the inside of my mask, seeping into my nose and mouth whenever I lay prostrate. Then there was that moment when I was lying at a parking lot exit that went out to a four-lane road where a car was insisting it needed to come out right that second, and the car owner and police and protest supporters converged into chaos while the person who happened to be lying down right in front of the creeping car was me. The protest organizers, who were the Solidarity Movement for No More Irregular Contracts, and the police noticed just in time and ran right up in front of the car to stop it, a fact I was told only later and am deeply grateful for. In the moment I was incredibly frightened, but my belief in the cause and my pride as a protester would not allow me to get up and run, so I had stuck my head into the asphalt and played dead instead.

And so, the Anti-Discrimination Act failed to pass, the Serious Accidents Penalty Bill became more and more compromised to the point of ruin, Staff Sergeant Byun Hui-su passed away, and twenty-three-year-old Lee Seon-ho died in an industrial accident at Pyeongtaek Harbor, with Lee Seon-ho's father, sister, and high school friends subsequently joining the labor rights struggle. A state of affairs so awful that I feel ready to jump into my next ritual prostration protest, whenever that may be.

In the midst of this, my publisher asked me if I had another short story similar to the mood of "The Center for Immortality Research," and I offered to just write them a new one, but I soon realized that with all the above going on, I was not in the right headspace to write another wacky comedic piece. I thought about it a bit more, and I happened to be reading the short stories of a Russian writer named Lyudmila Petrushevskaya. She was born in 1938 in Moscow, has been writing since the Soviet era, and is famous as a Russian postmodernist and woman writer. One of Petrushevskaya's most popular stories involves an old woman who writes all sorts of articles for various magazines and performs as a storybook reader for children, doing whatever she can to raise her grandchildren. Reading the story made me want to write a story centered on a similarly fierce old woman who narrates in an energetic and garrulous voice, and thankfully, the publisher ended up accepting "To Meet Her." I hope my readers find it acceptable, too, but a part of me does wonder if I'm only messing things up more for the real-life person the story is based on, regardless of my intentions.*

The only thing we can do now, it seems, is to endure. Until the pandemic is over, until the day we can breathe freely again, our only recourse is to survive the discrimination and violence and industrial accidents and deaths and loss and somehow endure.

* Staff Sergeant Byun Hui-su, the first out trans servicemember in the Republic of Korea military, underwent gender reassignment surgery while serving in the army and was subsequently discharged. She is thought to have ended her life in early 2021, and the Korean court ruled her discharge as unlawful in the same year. (Translator's footnote.)

"Maria, Gratia Plena" is a story I wrote in response to reading a newspaper article in 2018. It described an incident at a train station in the south of France where a male police officer shot to death his wife and two children with his police gun before killing himself. France is not known to be especially tolerant of domestic violence, and I hear they have a system in place that keeps victims and perpetrators apart. The wife of the policeman in question suffered domestic abuse for a long time, but because her husband was a police officer, it is said she did not have access to the proper channels of support—things are the same in every country, apparently. The wife had finally decided to take the children and run for their lives. The husband pursued them and murdered all of them. This happened a whole eighteen years into our enlightened twenty-first century. In 2020, a pandemic swept the world and we were not able to leave our homes. More women were beaten by their husbands, and more children were killed by the hand of their parents.

Just because I protest—following all the new rules such as continuing to move, and marches proceeding in socially distanced groups of nine—or ritually prostrate myself or sign online petitions or plant my face on the ground in front of the National Assembly or plant my face on the ground in front of the Blue House, it doesn't mean the world will change. There will still be those who will continue to be beaten in silence, and those who will continue to die in silence.

But maybe there will also be those who will survive. And I want to be able to have as little shame as possible when I stand before those who do. I protest and march and shout (with my mask on, but still) and sign and do push-ups down the street and lie down in front of a moving SUV so that I will feel at least a little less ashamed of myself. I protest for the sake of my own mental health and to preserve my own dignity as a human being. I need to be writing, but here I am, mostly protesting.

The German sociologist Karl Mannheim, in his book *Ideology and Utopia,* claimed that ideology was simply blather that did nothing to actually change society, and that utopian mentality was the true movement that could bring about change. He described four types of utopias. Let's ignore the Communist utopia, as they all petered out in the twentieth century. Next, there's the conservative utopian mentality, which asserts that utopia was already achieved in the past, and if we want a better world, we need to follow the examples of old. Then there's orgiastic chiliasm, an opaque term thanks to its Christian origins, but it basically means utopia must be achieved now and to do that we need revolution! Burn everything down! That kind of attitude. (Personally, I do like this one.) And there's the liberal humanist utopian mentality, which means the ideal society won't materialize in one's own lifetime, but we keep building toward it. I happen to know a lot of people who take this attitude to heart and give their everything to contribute to the coming of a better world. But the world also contains more or less an equal number of awful people as well. Sometimes, I am completely exhausted.

The Spanish philosopher Miguel de Unamuno y Jugo, in his book *The Tragic Sense of Life,* states that loss is the most significant characteristic of what it means to be human, and therefore the most human thing to do when faced with loss is not to move quickly to compensate or restore that loss but to pause and mourn. Andrei Platonov, a Russian novelist I love, also wrote that loss and trauma are the only common elements of human life, and all humans are connected through the mourning and trauma of loss, a common theme that emerges from reading much of his work.

Therefore, when faced with loss, one must mourn, and to remember and mourn loss, one must survive. If I do not remember, then who will remember those we have lost? And if I do not mourn through my actions, then how will I remember these losses?

Of course, the human memory has its limits. During the years the Sewol disaster protest site existed in Gwanghwamun Plaza and signatures were collected for the victims' families' petition, I thought I would never forget the names of the 304 who had perished. But now, I find myself uncertain of the class numbers of the Danwon High School students who were the majority of the Sewol victims. This is how fragile a person's memory is. Not to mention the fact that every day something happens to overwrite the tragedy that has come before.

Still, if I mourn and mourn with my body and soul, if I go out into the streets and act and try with what strength I have to make a difference for the sake of my survival and the survival of others, that can't be taken away. I will not be ashamed before the victims and their families, and we will be progressing slowly, very slowly but surely, toward a better world for both you and me—as we survive, and remember, and mourn.

—Bora Chung
Seoul, Summer of 2021